MW01121219

To PETER
BEST WISHES
Giovanni Rossi
2016

Clones
The Others

Giovanni Rocca

MR Comics & Art • Andover, Massachusetts

MR Comics & Art
5 Binney Street
Andover, MA 01810

Copyright © 2012 by Giovanni Rocca

All rights reserved. No part of this book may be used or reproduced in any manner whatsoever without written permission, except in the case of brief quotations embodied in critical articles or reviews.

Published 2012

ISBN 978-1-4675-3620-2

Book design by Kevin A. Wilson
Upper Case Textual Services
Lawrence, MA

Cover art by Giovanni Rocca

Clones: The Others

Introduction

Planet Earth is the home of humanity, created for them with a purpose. Humans have the power and the ability to create and to destroy. Earth is also the beginning of self-destruction. It is the destiny of humanity. The heart of man began to be evil and dark about 12,000 years ago.

In this chronological story of the human race, how human became so self indulged and tried to be gods and create things for their benefit, and to turn in a malice way to destroy itself. The imagination of man is vast. He wants more and more. He will not stop on what he desires. Curious and a self-proclaimed god, he will use his power with no care of what the consequences will be. The more science he endures the less of God's creation he will respect and expect. Man is not happy with himself. He is curious and full of questions.

This book is the second part of the *Clones* trilogy. It is the story of the Others, the second kind of clones. It tells us who they are and how they became what they are. Most books on science and astronomy tell us aliens are from outer space. Here you will find a different view of the Strangers—aliens, UFOs, and other phenomena.

This is a work of fiction from my own imagination. The idea for this story comes from researching, reading, studying the Bible, religion, the world of science, mathematics, history, geography, astronomy, medicine, geology, and physiology, as well as my personal feelings and knowledge.

I believe that fiction is just a way to distract the thoughts of humanity from reality. We ourselves come up with fantasy themes and stories, so people will get distorted and distracted from the reality of God and His creation. The life of humanity on planet Earth is a curse for some; for others it is a blessing. Whatever category fits you, you will have to decide what is good or bad. You have to separate truth from lies, the false from the real. You will decide!

This sci-fi story is the way I see the world and the human race. Aliens are from here, Earth, not from out there in space. Fiction? Yes. Reality? Maybe. Possibility? Who knows?

Read and read again. The more you read and study, the more knowledge you will gain, and that knowledge will take you to a point of no return. You will not be satisfied with what you have, with what you know and do. It is the goal of humanity to be able to transform itself.

In *Clones: Aliens or Us?* you read about the Strangers and discovered how they were created and the purpose of their mission. But you did not learn the reason for their creation. Why humanity decided to go so far was left a mystery. Is cloning the answer for a perfect human race?

The human race is on the brink of self-annihilation. Is this true science or just fiction? Just think if these imaginative thoughts would come true!

Humans are the only self-made gods and aliens. The desire they have is to control, to take over, to make, and to destroy. They will continue on with delusional thoughts and an evolving brain. They will process illusion and dreams to an extreme measure. It will be the end of society and race forever. Is this science fiction? Fact or reality? Keep your eyes on yourself; you will see how the change occurs every second, hour, day, month, and year of your life.

The question is, are we alone?

Or alone we are!

The Others

The aliens—that is, the Others—have left behind signs and instructions for humanity. The aliens intend for the human race and the planet Earth to self-destruct. They know the history of humanity. They know how man was created. They know that humans are weak and selfish, full of lies and malicious thoughts.

The aliens are the evil side of humanity. They will distort the way of humanity away from a belief in God to different religions and imaginations, toward confusion and the desire for power, to be like gods. Controlling the planet, the Others will use humans, making them like slaves. The Others will use and abuse them.

The aliens travel back into the past and forward into the future, for their ambition to distort humans and make them pay for creating the aliens. They know man, their evil accomplishments, and the direction man will take. The aliens are helping man to get there faster, from the beginning of man to the end of man. The aliens leave all kinds of unanswered questions, symbols, and sign: Nasca Lines, Stonehenge, Olmec, colossal heads, Stone Circle, Moa statues, pyramids, and other signs yet unknown to man. There are many new signs to be discovered. Once these new signs are uncovered and made known, then all will be revealed to the human race, the true knowledge, the outcome, and the fate of all.

The Universe: with no dimensions, infinite space. It is without beginning or end, constantly changing with new galaxies and planets. Life in the Universe is constant. It is not a place; it is an organism. The Universe and its composition make life possible, but bring both destruction and creation. With that, the planet Earth is the living star for all lives created from universal dust and the entire nuclear endeavor.

Planet Earth is the home for millions of species including humans. Earth is the only astronomical body where life is known to exist.

The planet was formed about 5 billion years ago. The Earth's biosphere constantly changes, with the atmosphere and other abiotic conditions on the planet enabling the proliferation of aerobic organisms as well as the formation of the ozone layer. These—together with the Earth's magnetic field—permit life to persist during this period and to exist for long time.

Beginning

A large object comes from the depth and darkness of space with great speed.

Unnoticed by man, it moves toward the Earth and stops, hovering near the Earth's moon. It is a large spacecraft, dark gray in color. The shape is square, and on the craft it has a multitude of cylinders resembling gears. It makes a roaring sound similar to a tremor. From inside the Others are monitoring the planet Earth. After observing, they discover life there in the form of plants, beasts, and other forms of life.

Sending down probes to investigate, they determine that the planet Earth is a haven of material. It is the source of their lives and their continuing existence in the Universe.

They descend with a small craft to investigate the planet that their maps indicate is Earth. Yes, they decide, this is what they were searching for.

The time they calculated is 4.5 billion years ago, back in a time when their mathematic calculations determined as the time to find Earth and begin their conquest of creation.

They have the capability to find all sorts of material, minerals and otherwise, for their survival, but they have need of a labor force to clean and purify all that they extract from the Earth.

The mother craft contains cells and DNA that remain from human testing and experiments that took place (or will take place) in the future. Taking from the mother craft all the cells from earthly creatures, they compose and fuse them together to develop a new creation, the outcome of their experiment: a new creation called A.P.E (Advanced Population Earthly). It is the first makeup of hominoids.

From then to a point 500 million years into the future, it evolves to the ape-man. The creativity of this new creation was almost non-existent. The brain does not evolved as rapidly as the aliens anticipated. It is a slow process.

With very little achievement or learning from that creation, the aliens become frustrated and short of patience. They leave behind that primitive time and travel into the future to see how the evolution of their creation has progressed. It is 150,000 years into the future.

They find a new and evolved world. The A.P.E were different, more human-like than what they left back in time. The new kind walked on two legs. They lived in more organized ways. Now they hunt for food. They don't cultivate or make things. They just live. They have no language or means of making decisions. Only a few routings. They live in caves. This evolved kind, which is from the aliens creation back 500 million years, live in an area marked "Africa" on the aliens' map.

The aliens depart from there, traveling to the future to the year 39,000 BC to convene their mission for the future of man. Now they see that the same line of A.P.E is more advanced. They not only hunt but also fish. They have clothes on their bodies. They live in caves and huts, new transformed living quarters. They eat raw food, fruits, and meat.

The aliens take one of the stronger males to their craft. They experiment with him, inserting a cell into the savage's cranium, and then send him back.

The savage wakes up. He looks around, then gets up. He walks with a drunken motion, searching for something. He grabs some sticks and dry grass, makes a bundle, and places it on the ground. Then he finds two stones and begins to scrape them together. Friction causes sparks to occur, igniting the bundle of sticks. The A.P.E. now has fire.

The aliens are impressed with their new accomplishment, and so they depart, travelling onward to the future to evaluate the progress through the millenniums to come and to shape humanity.

It is payback time!

The Brain

The human brain, the most complex organ in the body, is the center of the human nervous system. Enclosed in the cranium, the human brain has the same structure as that of other mammals, but it is about three times larger. Most of the spatial expansion comes in the cerebral cortex, a convoluted layer of neural tissue that covers the surface of the forebrain. Especially extended are the frontal lobes, which are associated with executive functions such as self-control, planning, reasoning, and abstract thought. Only humans have these abilities. A portion of the brain is devoted to vision. The evolution of the brain, from the early shrew-like mammal through primates to hominids, is marked by a steadily increasing encephalization, the ratio of the brain to body size. The number of neuronal and non-neuronal cells contain in the brain ranges from 75 to 90 billion.

These cells pass signals to each other through as many as 1,200 trillion synaptic connections. Due to evolution, the modern human brain has been shrinking over the past 18,000 years

Cain

The time is 12,000 BC or so, in the land of Middle East, which is part of the African world. There is a family working in the field. They have crops and animals to care for. It is a sunny day.

Two men are walking near the farm, going to their flocks of lambs. One man grabs a jaw bone of a donkey and hits the other man on the head until he is dead.

It is the first murder, the killer was Cain, and the dead one is Abel.

From above, inside their craft, the aliens are watching.

(Translate from their language.)

"That creature is what we are looking for. His qualities fit our needs. He is the right specimen for the experiment. We will name him Cain.

The aliens hold a conference with each other.

"We will see it, and we will commence our test and find out if it has the DNA we need."

From the craft, a blast of air shoots down to Cain. He becomes still. The aliens from the spacecraft speak to him.

"You … you did well. You will be the seed we need to evolve your mental superiority and teach you to create everything for your kind, for our benefit, and for the future of your species."

All of this takes place in a few seconds. Cain looks around but doesn't see anyone. He runs towards the desert in terror, screaming "Why? Why me?"

This is the first question.

He feels a sudden, brief feeling of sickness, a faintness. He runs until he falls on the hot sand, then turns with his face looking up at the heavens. And then he sees a brilliant, large black stone next to him. He moves towards it slowly and with great fear.

The stone on the sand is square. It looks like a tablet, cut perfectly with no flaws. It is inscribed in Arabic. He looks at it, but has no clue of what it is. An instant later, a loud sound emanates from the stone, and he faints.

When he comes to, he feels different—strange and stronger and smarter. He walks to the perfect block and reads the writing.

"This is magnificent; the writing on this stone is clear to me now. These seem to be instructions for the future of humanity. I will be the cause of the human race for major occurrences to come."

Cain walks for a long time in the desert. He comes across an encampment. The people look like him. They welcome him for dinner. And so Cain remains there for a long time. He marries and has children. With the aliens' instructions, he develops many things from housing, garments, and cook wear from all kinds of materials. He discovers the use of copper and iron, from which he creates weapons of all kinds. His knowledge grew by the day. His intellect is far superior to that of other men.

This is the first tribe and the first group of humans to use copper and iron. With the alien's help, they are able to use copper and iron long before humanity would have discovered them on their own.

The aliens see all of that and say, "It is all well ... he is on the right path that we had anticipated, and he will be the seed of knowledge for the Human race and to serve us."

From the seed of Cain the world multiplies with people. The Earth becomes populated with all kinds, both good and evil. Traditions are developed, new villages began, and different languages begin to be spoken. Disorganization and chaos began, from wars to the takeover of lands and properties, as well as killing, rape, and slavery. From then on, the human race is on a course to self-destruction.

"We can go for now we will return in a while to review his situation and labor."

With that they depart from the Earth's atmosphere at the speed of light, traveling through the solar system and our galaxy. Their optical sense instrumentation detect a shining light in a round form traveling in the opposite direction, speeding towards the Earth's sun.

"It looks as if it is a ball of gas," the aliens think.

The planet Earth continues in chaos, criminality, killing, destruction, and wars. In the years that follow, things go from bad to worse. The human race has no directions or instructions for the future. Time has gone by, with no new knowledge for the humans' future life. Cain creates an evil way of life. He manifests decay into immorality and corruption to his people. Now Cain is old and weary. In the meantime the aliens are traveling back to Earth to assess the progress and accomplishments of Cain. Orbiting the Moon to observe the Earth, they note that the planet is different from the first time they came.

"It seems different. A transformation took place here. It doesn't look the same. It's much greener then the first time"

They magnify the planet Earth and see nothing. The atmosphere is thick. The aliens study their advanced technological instruments, and finally acknowledge they are in a different solar system. It looks similar, but it is not the same as the planet Earth.

"For now we need to go back in time. This solar system is in the future. It is not of interest to us. We will return and foresee sometime in our future travels."

The aliens depart from there in a time warp, heading into the past.

Back in the time of Cain, new tribes emerge. More wars occur, malicious people are born and take over the land, and new knowledge and new ways of fighting emerges. Now there are kings and kingdoms. The aliens arrive there in the midst of a battle. They see humans fighting with themselves like animals—killing, burning, and decimating. They are glad of the outcome of their great experiment, with the human they call Cain serving as the first seed.

"Ha, here we are! Very good! There he is! Our seed!" one of the aliens says.

"No it is not him. He looks the same as the other one, it's true! But look closely. They are similar to each another, just as we designed our DNA experiment. Well done, seed Cain!"

They remain orbiting the Earth and monitoring the seed of Cain. They call him Can-aan, at their care. It doesn't matter who he is as long he will act according to their manifestation.

"There is a human growth. We shall go forth and continue our experiment with them. It is the time now."

So Can-aan was taken up onto their craft. They study him, the contour of his brain. They implant new cells of their own kind. After that they send Can-aan back.

"I had a strange dream! It is not possible!" Can-aan exclaims. Then he went on his way back to his tribe. He looks around him.

"I have a fantastic idea."

From that day on his ideas expand. The Tower of Babel is the first major construction of that time. Because Can-aan had the knowledge implanted in his brain, he designs great building and cities. The first cities of Sodom and Gomorrah are built, cities with a populous of immorality and failure. Crime and chaos flourish in them, but even they come to an end, giving humanity its first short glimpse of the future for man and the way he will go.

"We see that all is according to our plan," the aliens say.

Then they depart from there, continuing on their travels far into the Universe. In the meantime, on Earth distress accumulates, wars and confusion break out furiously. On top of all that, earthquakes, tornadoes, hurricanes, and floods are part of their punishment and destruction. The death of young people is terrible. Blood runs in streams and the flesh of humans and beast is mingled together everywhere.

Time passes and the aliens return. They decide to investigate in a new zone. They enter the Earth's atmosphere with a small craft, thirty kilometers in circumference, causing a bright light over the sky. They hover above the desert they call Egypt. From the craft an opening appears. Five of them float out from the inside. They observe a large crowd on their knees worshiping them like gods. They are a primitive race, frightened and confused at what was going on.

The spacecraft is so large and evil looking. Its roar is loud, raspy, and deep, with the smell of sulfur and melted metal.

The Pyramids

"Very well. This place is the right one. We can use it as the new central compass of this and other planets, for calculation of universal time to the four points of light. The humans will be useful in producing elements needed for the survival of our kind. We will take the female and implant our seed. They will have an incarnation of our looks and shape. It will be our offspring on this planet. We will collect the male and commence the map of our plans."

Then they study and form theories. They hypnotize the males. They line the men up one-by-one in five groups in a pyramid formation, a square design, pointing them to the sun in conjunction with the Moon. They call space kinetic energy, using the Earth and the human energy force to engage in building. From the spacecraft, a wave of invisible power travels across the desert to a far away mountain, cutting square blocks of granite with a precision cut and perfect measurements. One block after another floats above the sand. They place the blocks in an orderly manner inside the human design. All five buildings are completed at the same time without a single complication. They call them pyramids.

The First Pyramids

The Egyptians Pyramids are ancient masonry structures located in Egypt. There are about 138 of them. Most were built as tombs for the pharaoh and their consorts during the Old and the Middle Kingdom period. The earliest know Egyptian pyramid is found at Saqqara, northwest of Memphis. The earliest of these is the pyramid of Djoser built between 2630 and 2611 BC, during the Third Dynasty. The complex surrounding this pyramid is considered to be the world's oldest monument structure constructed of dressed masonry. The most famous Egyptian pyramids are those found at Giza. Several of the Giza pyramids are among the largest structures ever built. The Pyramid of Khufu in Giza is the largest pyramid still in existence.

Inside the pyramids are kilometers of tunnels in every direction. It is forbidden for the primitive to enter. Only the aliens have access to them. The pyramids are designed for the purpose of searching the stars, planets, and galaxies. They are not living quarters. Inside the five pyramids are scribes and directions. They are connected to a light source using the power of the sunrays. The five pyramids are used as navigational beacons. Two other pyramids are built: one for the stock-piling of minerals that the Earth supplied, which is collected by the primitives, while the other pyramid is used for the collection of sacrificial blood, human blood.

"Mission completed. We will return in one year (one hundred years primitive time) to collect the goods for our populace."

The aliens do not have a home planet. They live in the mother craft, which is about the size of the Earth's moon. They leave behind inscribed tablets with instruction for the primitives, so they will remember what to do: to find minerals that the aliens have discovered on Earth. They want and need these minerals and metals, including gold, silver, copper, carbon, sulfur, aluminum, magnesium, iron, and calcium for their neutron nuclear fusion.

To extract and clean all that, they need the primitives. Before departing from that area they called Egypt, they extract an initial sample of the minerals and metals to supply their craft. They assemble the primitive slaves together and transmit a message to them: "For now, we are in a good position and will be tranquil for a while, but we will return."

The natives fall on their knees and bow down to worship the aliens. The craft then departs into space.

The aliens build similar constructions in different parts of the world, in South America, Asia, and Europe. The purpose is the same: to use the natives as slaves to extract supplements from the Earth. Every one hundred years they will return to collect. For the Egyptians' labor, the aliens give them knowledge to advance in their social life, to become the first empire on Earth. They go on to build many great cities and over one hundred pyramids, including a line of twelve pyramids to serve as a calendar.

The Egyptians conquer the eastern part of the Earth with their might and knowledge. They become slave owners. With the slaves they build their mighty cities and extract minerals and metals for the aliens. They want to be ready when the aliens return to obtain them.

Each time the aliens return, they go from place to place making sure they don't run out of supplies. In every place and tribe they leave their mark, and with the native females they produce their offspring.

The aliens trash the planet Earth. They do the same to all parts of the Earth, from the Americas to Europe, Africa, and Asia, and to the four corners of the planet. They use the native to build the pyramids in different styles according to their needs. They use them to collect minerals and metals for many years, and then the pyramids become gifts for the primitives. They leave instructions and scripts on tablets to provide the natives with knowledge.

They name the people and cities according to their appearance. From the Egyptians to Mayas, Aztecs, Cholulas, and Zapotecs, the natives are the same. They are short with large faces, with large lips and nostrils. They have small, slanted eyes with a husky body.

In all these places the aliens build monuments of themselves of granite and different stones. The stones come from distant places. The aliens plan is to map and make a museum on Earth. From Egyptian monuments like the Sphinx, to the Olmec colossal head and Moai statues, the aliens sculpt them far from the cities. They cut them with precision and transport them to the place of their choice.

"It is done, for now. The ship is full. It is time to go. We will return soon for more."

This time they take a female and a male from each tribe to the mother craft for tests and experimentation.

At speed of light, they take off into the unknown. As they go, they observe the same thing as before: a bright light traveling faster than them toward the planet Earth.

Chaos

"The same thing again: the bright ball of gas going in the opposite direction. We don't need to be concerned now. We will investigate it in the future."

On Earth, confusion and chaos increases in the life of the humans day by day. The Egyptians are at war with the Babylonians to the East. In Africa, there is famine and death. In Asia, they overthrow kings and emperors. Killing and destruction are everywhere.

In the west, a new civilization emerges in Europe. The race calls themselves the Greeks. The Greeks are a different kind of people, nothing like the Egyptians, Asians, Africans, or Mayas. They are civilized in a different way. They are a white race with blue eyes, black and blond hair. They are tall with a muscular build, wearing beards. They are a society that will move the world into a vastly different dimension of knowledge and creation.

Even with their great civilization and advanced knowledge, the Greeks are at war with themselves, between the Spartans and Trojans. It is a bloodbath, a terrible way of life that continues for years. The Egyptians lost the power given to them by the aliens. Egypt can't produce any more supplies for the aliens, so they steal from and kill their neighbors. But it is a vain effort, as the Egyptians go from bad to worse. The year now is 3000 BC. In space the aliens' craft is orbiting and observing the planet Earth. They view the Egyptians, the Mayas, and all their creation and innovations with disappointment.

"These earthlings are a shamble ... wasted, worthless, disorganized, and confused. They are worthless for our use. We will give them a gift for all they have made, what they chose to change from what we did for them. We will go there and collect the supplies, and then visit all others for the exchange of gifts"

Since the last time they came, one thousand years have passed. They send down a large craft, which parks on top of the large pyramid to load the supplies.

The Egyptian pharaoh comes with his people to greet the aliens. From an opening six aliens come out. The pharaoh addresses them. "Great ones, we give you our respect and humbleness. We welcome you to this land. We are pleased to assist you and serve you again."

The alien look at each other and communicate tele-pathically, saying, "Disgusting. They are week and idiotic. We can't waste time with them!" Five of them return to the craft, but one remains. The one remaining looks at the pharaoh with anger.

"We are very, very sorry, my god. We don't have much. We did not have a good harvest this time. Things are not so good here. We are hoping that you will be pleased with what we have for you this time!"

The one that remain there wears a suit of strange material, charcoal gray with a golden belt. Small square plates are all over the suit: a chest plate in the form of a large star, blocks of square plates on top of each other. He wears something like boots on his feet. He floats on jets attached to the boots. He is about ten meters in the air, looking down at the natives of Egypt. Slowly, he puts his hands to his head and removes his head gear, which is also decorated with the squares made of gold, silver, and precious stones. He strips of out of the space materials. He has a look of evil.

As he removes his head gear, for the first time the native see the features of the alien's face.

"My god, you have the same features as us!" the Pharaoh exclaimed.

The alien comes close to them. His looks have the features of the sphinx and olmec. His black eyes bear Asian traits. He has a large, flat, African nose, a square face, and a large head. He stands one and a half meters tall.

The alien becomes angry with them.

"Please forgive us if you are displeased, my greatest god!" the pharaoh exclaim with fear.

In the Egyptian language, the alien said "I am not your god. I am your destiny."

He places his hand on his chest, pushing on the star. The star begins to rotate. It snaps from the breast plate and flies in a circling motion in the direction of the pharaoh, killing him. It is the beginning of their use of force and a demonstration of their ability to destroy. The natives have no idea of the aliens' powers.

The other metal parts from his suit also disengage. Flying at the speed of sound, they kill more people. Chaos and terror are in the midst of Egypt. People are scared and confused. They panic in horror at the aftermath. About one thousand Egyptians are dead, but not one drop of blood is visible.

"Our work is done here. We will return soon. If things are the same, the lesson shall be even harsher."

The natives receive new instructions on how to bury the dead and to use selective herbs on the body. They learn to cover them with a special cloth that will preserve the dead bodies for future experiments that the aliens will perform. They are also given instructions on how to obtain more supplies.

The aliens depart in the same craft and travel to the Americas, to the land of what they called Mayas. They descend to the tall pyramid where they park. As in Egypt, they begin to collect the goods. But they notice something was wrong here as well. The native Mayans are a bit more advance than the Egyptians, but here too there seems to be an aberration. A new generation has learned to live differently. They have a different organization. They worship the sun as a god, and called themselves the sons of the sun.

The aliens find the cistern empty, without goods. The natives are united in a crowd to welcome the aliens. The aliens know that what they have is only part of the supplies. With anger, disappointment, and a shortness of patience, they look out over the people.

"These good for nothing savages! They shall be

exterminated immediately." In a split second, the aliens come to a conclusion: they will need their blood.

"We will come back. We will make sure they will have the blood we need for our survival."

The Mayans wait for some kind of reaction from the aliens, but what they get are instructions detailing how to produce blood and preserve the blood in special containers that the aliens give them. For their punishment, they have to sacrifice their first-born males.

The aliens orbit Earth for years, and then depart. It will be a long time until they return.

Blood Sacrifice

The aliens return in a year to collect the blood from the Egyptians and the Mayas because they are the closest to their DNA. They also come for minerals and supplements. They use a new kind of people that the aliens call Aztecs and Incas. The aliens build other type of pyramids and temples and statues of themselves. Everywhere there are images of them. The natives collect a multitude of supplies, including gold, silver, and minerals of all kind. The aliens experiment with the natives, both humans and animals, for their amusement. They split cells. They mix DNA and insert their own cells and DNA into them. And so new creatures are made. Some look like humans with the heads of eagles, cats, cobras, and oxen. Some of them have the back of their skulls elongated. They speak with superiority over the older natives. They are tall, slender, and strong. The aliens place these new creations in Egypt. The natives worship them like gods. These creatures rule Egypt with the help and the power of the aliens. They sculpted monuments of themselves.

The aliens return to the Maya. The Mayans do not provide as much blood as the aliens had demanded. There is very little there, but the aliens are willing to wait for a little while longer, because the Mayas' blood is very important for their kind. So, they call the chief of the tribe. "We will help you to meet our requirements. We will teach you how to extract your blood."

With new temples, the Mayans learn to sacrifice more efficiently. The aliens build columns with precision measurements. Holes on the columns align with the stars in Orion's belt. The aliens give the Mayas a calendar to mark the passage of time for the aliens to travel into the future and into the past any time. They also give them knowledge of the future of the human race to confuse the human system. All of this occurs about 3000 BC, when the aliens began with the Mayas.

After the aliens are done with them, they take off to the mother craft. There, the aliens have a conference.

"For the good of our kind, for our progress and our survival, we can't leave this planet. The resources are vast, and we can use any of these natives for the labor and production."

They return to the past to visit the Egyptians, to see their situation and to collect supplies, but there is nothing more. The time comes when the aliens decide to make an end of the Egyptians, eradicating their lifestyle and their laziness.

"This action will be recorded on their history tablets. From this destruction a new race will be born"

A jolt of an enormous energy comes down from the craft. It causes a nuclear explosion. One third of the population dies, and one third of Egypt is buried under a cloud of sand. The only thing visible is three pyramids.

The same fate befalls the Babylonians and part of their world and people. No trace of any kind of history was visible. All becomes a blur. All of this occurs at warp time (the aliens' time).

They will come and go at any time they want. The people of the Earth will never know of their traveling back and forth, to and from the planet Earth.

Twelve thousand years into the future, they return. This time they see what they started in the past, from their first seed, Cain.

The mother craft stops and orbits near planet Mercury to observe what's happening on Earth. The year is AD 2009 of human time.

"This is the fruit of our experiment. It is according to our plans. It is going the way we designed it for the natives of this world."

The human race has advanced in gruesome ways with knowledge beyond their own imagination, even with experiments of their own. The aliens then travel back in time to AD 1932. They find a new revolution in science. The place is Germany, and the new science is cloning. The aliens know that it is the way they predicted.

"So far so good," they exclaim. "They need our help to make it possible, so it will be right and complete for the future of our existence."

They go down with a small craft. They paralyze the scientists and penetrate into their brains, manipulating their cells, implanting their brains with particles from the aliens' own cells, which provide the scientists with the knowledge needed to perform the task for the aliens' conquest.

"We have good specimens in this part of the planet. What we need is a new seed to continue our work to steer humanity along an evil way."

With gleeful laughter, one human comes to their mind: Hitler.

"He is the seed from the blood line of Cain and Caesar Caligula. We will develop his knowledge and expand his abilities beyond all other things we have done." So they take Hitler into their mother craft and place him on a contraption. They work on his cerebellum in a microscopic way. Afterwards, they transport him back to Earth.

They go back to mother craft and depart, traveling at the speed of light into the past. This time they go back to Africa for their final collection of goods. But they find misery. There is nothing much to collect from the Africans. By then, Africa is a powerful empire, large and strong but was short lived.

The aliens descended from the mother ship in a shuttle and park the craft above the large pyramid. The craft is a large one, about 10 km square. The Africans look up in fear, motionless with terror and panic. In dismay some of them scatter, while others kneel to worship the aliens. But this time, the situation is different. A blast from the craft slices the ground like a nuclear explosion without fire, destroying buildings and exterminating the people. It is the end of Africa.

It becomes a desert of sand. All is buried beneath. Only

the tip of one pyramid is showing. After the destruction of Africa, they depart to warp into the future.

"We will travel back to 3666 BC to find the natives of Maya. They shall be waiting for our arrival and have all the supplies that we instructed them to collect."

When they arrive there, they find a large celebration of a victory against another tribe. This is the empire of the Sons of Sun, advanced with knowledge given by the aliens to the Mayas to build their great cities and monuments, with large pyramids and statues of the aliens in every building for worship.

The Mayas

The Mayas are a Mesoamerica civilization, noted for having the only known fully-developed writing system in pre-Colombian America, as well as for its art, architecture, mathematics, and astronomical system. It was initially established during the pre-Columbia period 2000 BC to AD 250 according to the Mesoamerica chronology. Many Maya cities reached their highest state of development during the classic period AD 250 to 900, and continued to the post-classical period. The Mayan civilization shared advances such as writing, epigraphy, and a calendar, which we know did not originate with the Mayans, but their civilization fully developed them.

The End of a Race

When they saw what had happened, they became irritated with the Mayas for their lack of respect and failure to produce what the aliens expected from them.

"These natives are brainless beasts. They will be exterminated. We no longer have a use for them"

With anger and frustration, they make a decision for extermination.

From the craft a jolt of energy like a tornado kills two-thirds of the natives and destroys ninety percent of all buildings. They are buried under soil. No trace of them is recorded. The same fate befalls the Aztecs and Incas.

The aliens then travel to Africa. There they expect the goods to be prepared and ready for transport to the craft. In an earlier time, after they had scouted the continent, they called Africa the land of plenty. They also use the natives to build structures like pyramids, in conjunction with all the others in different part of the globe for their on purpose. The aliens discover that Africa is rich with minerals, including diamonds, a new mineral that will be one of major importance for the alien's survival and progress.

Using the natives of Africa, the aliens extract one-fifth of the solid rock from the ground and mountains, leaving craters like volcanoes and deep holes on the terrain. Finally, the aliens acknowledged that there was little more to reap, so they decided to go on to a different site. The aliens were good to the natives of Africa. They left them to survive on their own. The aliens fill the holes with water and leave some of the buildings for them. The Africans prosper for a while, but slowly the population began to deteriorate. Agriculture decreases and can no longer sustain the people. Thousands of people die of diseases and hunger, without the knowledge needed to produce medicine. They cannot sustain life.

From the mother craft, the aliens observe the eastern continent of Earth. They discover a land of a people with very small frame. They call them Chinese.

"They look more like us," one of them exclaims. "We will survey the area, and then enslave them for their goods. We will mold them to be like us."

One other agrees.

They begin to use them. They abduct women and insert their alien DNA in their wombs for incubation, resulting in millions of new births. As with the Egyptians and the Mayans, they use them to extract raw materials. They instruct the Chinese to build temples and monuments. They give them knowledge to produce a black explosive powder. The aliens remain with the Chinese for a while until they collect enough goods.

"We will return for more. Be prepared! For your sake, you want to make sure our return does not find a lack of gathered goods," they exclaim to the emperor.

They depart to the mother craft. At the council, the aliens meet to have a forum to reach a decision.

"The decision of the council is to send six ships to eradicate the entire resources that Earth supplies. It is necessary now."

They send the ships all around the Earth. One of the craft orbiting Europe above the area of Scotland observes the land and sees the people there. The aliens are bewildered. They don't understand. The native there are different from them. This is the first time they see this white race.

"For the depth of the Universe, what kind of humans are these?"

They inform the mother craft of the scenario. The mother craft moves to survey and probe the land itself. After probing all the British Islands and not finding any kind of goods, they go down to meet the natives. Thousand of them gather, looking up at the craft. The spectrum of light shining down on them hypnotizes them. They remain still, paralyzed. From the mother craft, the message is delivered to use the natives to build the clock for the aliens. The aliens maneuver the natives one-by-one, making six circles inside one another, creating a ripple effect. The monument is called Stonehenge. It is aligned with the planets with four entrances. It was also used as a temple by the natives for the worship of the aliens. They cut the stones far away from the area, a distance of fifty kilometers. After the aliens cut the stones, they bring them to the site. Then the stones are put together. The aliens elevate each stone, placing them one-by-one where each native stood. It happened so quickly that the natives never knew what occurred.

The aliens depart from England, leaving the natives with no additional knowledge for their advancement. They go to other places there, but find nothing of any use to them. They decide to return there after a time warp into the future, for a possible transformation of the land of Britannia.

The aliens use humans because of the kinetic powers the humans possess. They use this system for all their missions.

Stonehenge

Stonehenge is a prehistoric monument located in England, county of Wiltshire, about 3 kilometers (2 miles) west of Amesbury and 13 kilometers (8 miles) north of Salisbury. One of the most famous sites in the world, Stonehenge is composed of earthworks surrounding a circle of large standing stones. It is at the centre of the most dense complex of Neolithic and Bronze Age monuments in England, including several hundred burial mounds. The surrounding circular earthen bank and ditch have been dated about 3100 BC.

In the mean time, the second scout craft is orbiting the skies above Italy, where they had built a pyramid for the natives of Italy at a site called Montevachio. The aliens know that land is rich in a particular mineral, a material called marble. It is soft granular carbon from volcanic eruptions. For the aliens, that material is an ingredient used for some of their ships' structure. The aliens built a pyramid there also, but it was of a little significance because the natives of Italy were a more advanced race than the others natives. The message delivered to them from the mother craft was to find the richest man there and to transport him to the mother craft.

They discover that these natives are very different from all the others that they had engaged with in the past. "These natives don't look like us. They are a different breed, but this man is the same kind as the first savage we used in the past. Perhaps he is from the same seed."

The man that they adopted was the ruler of that people there. His name was Romulus. He was to be the DNA line of the Romans.

"This man is superior. His brain has developed far more than all other men on Earth. We will use and instruct him to become the leader of a grand and important empire, which will bring about big changes for the human race."

They transport Romulus back to his quarters. The aliens then depart from Italy to return in the future.

Romulus rules Italy for few years. He names that land Rome. With the knowledge given to him by the aliens, the empire was born. Under his control, new constructions, inventions, medicine, mathematics, astronomy, and above all the search for minerals become a daily task for the natives. Their labor is for the glory and growth of Rome.

"We have done well with him. We will depart from this time and return in the future."

Marble

Marble is a rock resulting from metamorphism of sedimentary carbonate rock. Limestone dolomite causes variable re-crystallization of the original carbonate mineral grains. The Italian Sienese marble is yellow or yellowish-white and the Carrara marble is white or blue-gray.

Twenty years pass, then the alien craft arrives to supply the craft with the goods. Romulus is prepared for them. The supplies are all there waiting for them. The aliens return a few more times to collect their supplement. The aliens recognize the brainpower of this race and the power to accomplish.

"With harmony we see your future."

"Yes. Your race will be the mightiest power on Earth."

"The blood line commences with you, Romulus."

With endurance, grand courage, and superior knowledge, Romulus responds, "I will. I will, master. My people will follow."

So the power of the Roman race begins it grand dominion, conquering the world for a thousand years with no mercy. In their path, they leave destruction and death, as well as their superior knowledge of engineering, especially in building roads and bridges. They are advanced above all other races. Their military power is unstoppable. The objective of the aliens is to have a powerful race control the planet so the aliens can control the inhabitants of the Earth.

Through Romulus and his bloodline and the implantation of genetic engineering with the aliens DNA, the

Roman Empire is a prestigious creation for the future of the human race for millenniums to come.

Rome conquers the world, expanding civilization. It marks the foundation of government and laws.

Rome

Rome's early history is shrouded in legend. According to Roman tradition, the city was founded by Romulus in 753 BC. The legendary origin of the city tells that Romulus and his brother Remus decided to build a city. After an argument, Romulus killed his brother. Archaeological evidence supports the view that Rome grew from pastoral settlements on the Palatine Hill built in the area of the future Forum and later expanded under the Republic and then the Empire. The broader history of the Roman Empire extends sixteen centuries and includes several stages in the evolution of the Roman state. It encompasses the period of the ancient Roman Empire, the period of division into western and eastern halves, and the history of the Eastern Roman or Byzantine Empire that continued through the Middle Ages and to the beginning of the Modern Era.

New Race

Claudius Augustus Caesars is the emperor after the death of Romulus. The Empire begins to stretch from all of Italy to the north, south, west, and east.

"We are satisfied with all you have accomplished and all the resources you collected for us."

"You and your people will prosper. We will give you more and more knowledge to conquer any place on this planet."

"Everything you do and invent will multiply your creativity year after year. No one will conquer you"

Claudius responds with a question.

"We Romans have received your instructions. What do we need to do to maintain relations with you?"

The aliens respond, "Contributions from you, for our need, at any time we need them. Do this, and we will give you more power and knowledge."

"You will have resources from all other natives of this planet," he replies.

At the same time, the other spacecraft around the planet creates different signs throughout the planet to serve as navigational guides for their return to Earth. They know that the Earth and the human race will change in dramatic and spectacular ways.

All of this occurs because of the Roman transaction. It will impact the Earth, for generations to come.

The aliens then leave the Earth and return to the mother craft. They depart Earth's atmosphere.

"What is that? It looks the same ball of gas that we see every time we go away from this planet" The aliens confer about the object. "Is this signifying anything that needs to concern us?"

The aliens dismiss the sphere of light for the third time, again with no understanding of its significance and meaning. Throughout the centuries, the Romans hold dominion over the Earth by killing, stealing from villages and cities, and taking all the possessions from Egypt and Africa, and from all corners of Europe. An unstoppable regime, they go on for two thousand years.

The command from the aliens to the Romans was that their task is to go and spread what they know. They are to build the Empire in every part of the planet Earth and its population.

The aliens first began with the Greeks, but they collapsed after a short period. Problems of competition and selfish kingdom between the Trojans and the Spartans led them to conquer each other, so the aliens created a much larger empire, the Persian Empire, to supersede the Greeks. It was the end of a civilization, for the Persians also came to an end. For them it was a temporary empire, used only for the aliens' manipulation of the human o race. The aliens created a new species of human, clones of themselves used to help the Persians, but even for the alien clones it came to an end.

After a thousand years, the Romans see no sign of the aliens. They seem to have disappeared from the face of the Earth. The knowledge given to them has become stagnant. They make very few advances. Only the Romans maintain prosperity and growth, and continue collecting goods for the aliens.

The world is changing. It is going from bad to worse. Without new knowledge humanity is confused and lost.

Generations pass. The future is gloomy, with no hope for the human race. From Egypt to the Mayas, Africa, Asia, and the Americas are in chaos. Humanity slowly forgets the aliens and what they have done for the planet Earth and to the humans. With short memory, humanity creates its own kind of alien creature, completely off track. Confusing and complex ideas lead them astray. They have nothing but imaginations of images for years to come.

In space, millions of light years from Earth, the aliens are traveling at speed of light, searching other planets for the possibility of new discovery for their needs and to manifest their creation.

"We have been traveling for a long time from galaxy to galaxy. There is no sign of life like that on Earth. We shall go back and visit the Romans to collect more supplies."

AD 51 sees new rulers for the Roman Empire, from the crazy Caligula to the evil Nero. Everything is different. Rome is the richest country, while the rest of the world continues in poverty, hunger, disease, and barbaric wars. No one is safe.

The aliens return, hovering near the Moon again, watching the Earth and the Romans. What they see makes them angry.

"This empire is getting weak!"

"Looks like we will not collect anything here. That creature called Caligula is not what we need."

"We will use him for the end of the Roman Empire"

"But before we do that, a lesson needs to take place there."

They observe a place that the Romans love called Pompeii. Pompeii is the cream of the crop for Roman paradise, a secret place for leisure.

"We will destroy this place."

Pompeii. It is a calm night. All is well. From above, the mother craft sends a blast of air to Mount Vesuvius. The mountain ignites, sending an explosion high into the sky, causing a grand earthquake. Fumes and ashes are scattered for miles, destroying Pompeii and bringing death to all living things. The people have no chance to escape from the city. Only a few Romans survive, the witnesses of the terror that took place there.

With the devastation of their great and beautiful city, the Romans suffered great depression. That point marks the beginning of the fall of the Romans.

Now the year is 1452. The Romans are still an advanced race and a productive country with inventions and creativity, while the rest of the world is in shambles. Wars, revolutions, no growth in medicine or agriculture. Famine, disease, and death take their toll.

At the same time in Italy, a child is born: Leonardo

di ser Piero da Vince. He grows up to be the only human with a superior mind, the only one with any imagination.

"That man is superior to any of the others we have studied in our time on this planet! Something has occurred. We missed what happed here. Let us go back to investigate the past to determine how this came about."

The aliens time warp into the past. They search through the years of their absence, but they come up empty-handed. Confused and disoriented, they return to the year 1462, a miscalculation. They know that the boy, Leonardo, is conducting experiments in a different ways with different knowledge, a knowledge that was not from the aliens. Leonardo is engaging in new ways of doing science, medicine, art, invention, and mathematics.

"Something is strange here. Let us go on to the future for more information. Then we will come back to undo this new knowledge."

They depart from the Earth into the darkness of space.

Extraterrestrial Intelligence

Leonardo da Vince (Leonardo di ser Piero da Vince) was born in Florence, Italy, on April 15, 1452. Leonardo was one of the greatest painters and sculptors. He was a scientist, musician, inventor, engineer, mathematician, geologist, writer, and architect. A person with a one of the greatest minds in the history of the world, his curiosity for the creation and God made him what we know today as a Renaissance man.

Leonardo became one of the most important men for the future of humanity. His knowledge changed the way humans approach experiment and invention. The question is, who gave him this new knowledge?

Time goes by, and day-by-day the change is grand beyond human understanding.

The aliens return to Earth in 1951.

"This world is different. It has new knowledge. They have made great advancements in construction and life."

"We did not do this."

"It looks different. There is a force here in rapid motion."

"We need to find the cause."

What the aliens see in that era is a prosperous time for

the human race in fantastic ways. The world is a peaceful place, a loving society of intelligent people. The aliens travel to the year 1480. There they see Leonardo on a balcony, looking at the sky and sketching on paper. They acknowledge his wisdom.

"We understand now. He is designing a conventional system in a schematic way for the future of his fellow men."

"We did not give it to him!"

"Who, then?"

Then the aliens communicate telepathically. They are very angry. They want to kill Leonardo and destroy all his sketches and ideas, so they can have someone different to do their work and carry out their design.

"No!" The elder, whose name was Me, says. "We can use him for the good of our kind. He can manifest new inventions on our behalf."

They put Leonardo to sleep and implant new thoughts in Leonardo's mind. When he comes to, his first idea is to design gears, a new mechanism. With these, the world changes. It begins to proceed in the way the Others expected.

The others then travel to the future, to the year 1915, the time of the First World War. There they see the fruits of the new design implanted in Leonardo. They are satisfied with the direction humanity is taking.

They observe the humans and their progress once more with a distasteful feeling at the turn around in their lifestyle.

"Here we are. This forsaken race shall pay for our creation!"

"Yes, for what they have done to us!"

"Devastation, horror, and chaos for years to come!"

"Their logic will lead to self-extermination!"

"Let us help them with new ideas. We will teach them more malicious ways of destruction."

So wars, destruction, diseases, and famine wreak havoc upon the Earth. The human race goes from bad to worse for the next 3 years. When the war ends and a new life begins, the time of turmoil ceases for a while. For the next 22 years, the Earth changes again with new inventions, buildings, transportation equipment, machines, and evil weapons, all of which transformed humanity's way of functioning. Now they are more powerful and advanced, ready for bigger and more devastating machines of destruction. There is no turning back; it is too late. Their intelligence and wisdom are in conflict with each other.

Confused and dismayed, humans look toward a gloomy future.

The inventions and sheer amount of study from Leonardo has brought the advancement of knowledge. The human race changes the world at a rapid pace, some for good and some for evil. But in a short time, it becomes destructive and malicious. Humans glorify themselves with their new knowledge, but lack understanding of its origin.

In the years that follow, humans accomplish many marvel advances in medicine and science. The greatest of all is the mapping of the world. From the Romans to the New World, the Americas, a geometric and geographic evolution allows humans to travel farther and faster. The invention of machines and optics leads to innovations in telescopes and satellites. Communications become almost instantaneous throughout the planet. The consequences are daunting. With more inventers, people begin to make more and more things. Eventually, it leads to the study of nuclear fusion and so to the creation of the atomic bomb.

Nuclear Fusion

Nuclear fusion is a process of chemistry, physics, and astrophysics where two or more atomic nuclei fuse together to form one nucleus accompanied by the release or absorption of a large quantity of energy. The first human project to experiment with fusion was the Manhattan Project in 1940, but it was not successful until 1951. In November 1952, the Ivy Mike hydrogen nuclear fusion explosion tests were carried out.

The others, the aliens, spend the time traveling at the speed of light in the Universe. They stop at a new galaxy they named H.6.F.

"This place is formed just likes the Earth's galaxy"

"It doesn't appear to have any life."

"Let us send a probe down to investigate."

The planets are large. Some have four rings, others have many moons. Some have large holes. One is like a ball of snow, while another is black like the night. Millions of meteoroids float and strike against one another.

At one planet, the probe penetrates the planet for an investigation. When the aliens find nothing they cause a thermonuclear explosion, shooting hot lava into space at speed of sound, leaving the planet's atmosphere and continuing into the infinity of the Universe.

"There is no life or material for our use here."

"We will circle this galaxy before we return to Earth."

The hot lava from that planet travels with speed into space. Cooling, it become mass of iron in all shapes (what we know as meteorites). Once these meteorites reach Earth, scientist from all corners of the planet begin to study them, bringing about another leap forward in technology for the human race. The advancement is extraordinary. Technology increases by the year on a grand scale. Humans feel they are on the top of creation and in control, taking charge of everything on the planet. But they calculate wrong. The most malicious invention is the atomic bomb, and the most horror comes from its subsequent use. From 1932 to 1938, the Germans develop amazing machinery and military power. They are ready for to take over the world.

But now, the aliens return to Earth.

"This German race will do well for us."

"They have a strength and knowledge similar to the Romans."

"They will conquer the world with their new equipment and new technology"

The aliens give Hitler the mind and character of an insane scientist and controller, creating chaos for the human race.

The same thing takes place in countries like Russia, Japan, and the United States. Symbols of power are given to each of them. For the Germans, it was the swastika and the SS. They called themselves the Third Reich, meaning the third line of change from Cainto Claudius Augustus to Hitler.

Controlled by the aliens, Hitler wreaks havoc in Europe. Europe is in the chaos of World War II. The devastation of the next three years is horrific, with millions of people dead. The aliens see that it is a good method for the slow extermination of the human race. This is the beginning of the end for humanity.

"The progress is vivid."

"We will continue with our quest for the future of these humans."

"Before we engage in that, we will place a new horror on them."

"We have chosen the location."

The others travel to America, to the year 1920, when the country was progressing in agriculture. People are getting land at very low cost to cultivate and produce food for the world. The aliens help them with new inventions, and the people of America develop new machines to speed up production to the point of self-destruction. It continues for ten years of growth, with a great economy. All is good. The country begins to supply the world with grain, the element of life and prosperity. The farmers of America flourish for the ten-year period.

"It is time for deliver the horror to these self-glamorizing humans."

From their craft, they manipulate the temperature over Oklahoma, causing draught for a month. Crops and animals begin dying every day. There is no rain in their future. The aliens follow this with a blast of air that hits the ground with a fantastic force, creating a strong wind that causes a wall of dust as high as 10,000 feet, moving at the speeds of 40 to 85 miles an hour, destroying everything. The dust storm covers many states, from the plains of Oklahoma to Colorado, Texas, and Kansas, and reached as far as the northeast of the country. The dust causes death, disease, hunger, and a horrible economic depression for ten years.

The war came and went, but the trouble was just starting for humanity. With new weapons and advanced science, the situation continues to deteriorate. Russia becomes the Red Army, the terror of Eastern Europe. They are no different than the Germans. The aliens use them just like they used Hitler and the people of Germany. Now they have a new country and its people to make into a superpower, giving them new knowledge in science and mathematics. The Russians develop new types of destructive weapons. They intend to conquer the world, beginning with Eastern Europe.

The aliens at this time are observing the planet Earth from the mother craft.

"It is time to direct the second superpower, the United States, with a grand new technology."

So it happens; they use this new country to spread the seed of evil. It begins earlier in time, before it was America. This continent is vast with prairies, valleys, and deserts. It is the perfect place for the aliens to experiment and fulfill their needs. It has a small population. The aliens look all around, but there are only a few groups and villages, inhabited with people who have primitive technology, who only live by the day.

"We see it has the potential to extract what we seek."

"We need people to do the work. We will bring them from other places."

And so they begin directing people from the east and west, and in particular a man that the aliens knew would make an amazing change to the world and the human race. From the first day when Christopher Colombo put foot on this land and called it America, everything changed. It changes by the day. More and more people settle in this vast country, looking for a better future than what they would have in Europe.

"This continent is good for us."

"It will produce all the supplies we need."

"We will use these new people for the labor. We will help them to become the greatest nation in all prospective matters and the most advanced in all fields. They will be the superpower of the world."

America through the years became the place to be. Every human being dreamed of residing in this new country, the New World.

The country grows slowly. The means of transportation are hard and harsh. By the time the people arrive in the land of plenty, there are more people dead than alive. They bring with them all kind of diseases.

The aliens see all of that, and they become angry.

"We need to speed up the process!"

The aliens from the mother craft began to search the planet. They decide to use people from Africa for the labor in America.

"There is the answer."

They travel to Europe. There are people working the ground and fishing using boats. So they brain-wash the sea merchants and send them to Africa to collect natives to be used as forced labor. Thousands of young boys and girls are taken from Africa to the New World, America. The same scenario had occurred thousands of years back.

Crop Circles

The aliens time warp into the future to 1951. They spot strange circular designs and formations.

"What are these?"

"They must be some strange new technology unknown to us."

Confused and dismayed, they search for answers. They study their planetary map of the Universe: galaxies, nebulas, and black holes. They travel into the past and future, but they cannot discover the origin of the crop circles.

Crop Circle

Crop circles or crop formations are not always the same shape. No one knows when they began. The first recorded accounts of them are from the late 1960s and early 1970s. They consist of patterns formed by flattening wheat, rapeseed, rye, maize, and/or barley. Thousand of crop circles have been reported over the world, ranging in size from small circles to large circles. The largest number of circles has been reported in England. Some people believe they are made by aliens, while others claim they are nothing but hoaxes.

America is at a time of population growth with very little technology. They are struggling for their survival. The year is around 1500. The advancement of life is slow in coming, and for over 200 years the aliens collect very few supplies from the planet.

"It is time for the increase of human labor in this part of the planet so we can have the goods."

And so, it comes the time for the labor force to increase. From 1750 to 1850, the aliens collect plenty of goods from the Americas. They leave the country in chaos with more problems, including the killing of people and civil wars. The living conditions are gloomy and evil. Starvation and diseases take a toll on this new country for about 100 years.

When the aliens return to Earth, the year is 1945. The planet is deep in World War II.

"Again and again! These humans are great for us! They perform well!"

"It is a good entertainment."

"Let us play a game with them!"

From the mother craft, they see the perfect people with whom to play their game: a small island and its people, whom they previously named Japa-ness (from the Egyptian/Mayan creation). The aliens infuse their brains with aggression. They are very enthusiastic for death, to attack America, and for self-destruction.

The game continues and escalates to a major attack by America on the island of Japan. The Americans now have their new weapon of mass destruction, but they don't want to use it. The power of the atomic bomb, discovered by

Einstein and Fermi with the help of the aliens, will be the number one problem for humanity.

"What is going on with them?

"Let us help them to make the decision."

The aliens use countries like pawns. They play their game by placing strategic information into the leaders of different countries as well as army generals. This information leads them to dream of conquest and control. This time, it will be a major devastation, so first the aliens use the small country of Japan to initiate an attack on the big and powerful country of America.

"We will take America first," the leader of Japan announces with malice and arrogance. "Then Europe!"

He is secure, and he thinks it is just.

Japan makes plans for the attack on Pearl Harbor, the home station of the American navy in the Pacific. The best of the Japan's air force departs from Japan to strike and to deliver devastation to the Americas.

The aliens abduct President Truman and take him to the mother craft. They plant all the information that the aliens want him to have, knowing it will lead him to the use of the atomic bomb to destroy thousands of Japanese. It is the first major destruction for the human race and the world

Atomic Bomb

The atomic bomb was one of the most devastating human weapons invented for two reasons: its destructive capability and its power. In 1945 during World War II, the United States by order of President Harry S. Truman dropped two bombs three days apart on the Japanese cities of Hiroshima and Nagasaki. Within two to five months of the detonation of the nuclear bombs, the death-toll was around 250,000. The cities were demolished to ground level. The Japanese surrender soon followed in September 1945. This was followed by the production of larger and more destructive nuclear bombs by many countries.

"This time they asked for it. We will not retreat or dismiss these outrageous acts. It is time to stop this nonsense of war."

One evil thing after another will be the gain for humans and their knowledge. The aliens are destructive and full of vengeance. They will use the humans for their own needs. They will bring them to self-destruction. This is the aliens' scheme. Humanity doesn't know of what is coming.

Every time the aliens return to Earth, some major environmental disaster occurs, with a multitude of death and diseases. Humans try to fix them, but end up making things worse. They are infected with the aliens' malice. They can't make it better. The aliens travel the Universe to conquer other planets, and every time they depart Earth they observe again and again the bright ball. They begin to take interest in this phenomenon.

"It is strange that we see this star come at speeds that are unknown to us. We need to research and take an interest in finding out what it is."

"Could be something extraordinary that is against us?"

"Is there possibly a confrontation in the near future?"

"Is it possibly a new species with greater knowledge than we have?"

But their concern is short-lived. They do not see any possible danger for the moment.

Some time goes by. The Earth looks good and the humans are doing well. They have amazing inventions, their health is good, and their advancement in technology is in great shape. From afar, the aliens monitor the humans and their progress. They don't like what they see.

"Something is going on down on planet Earth with the earthlings."

"They have a new knowledge that is somewhat different than ours."

"These new brain cells with which they progress do not come from us."

"Something is wrong here."

"Investigation is needed."

'We will send a craft down and collect some humans and test them."

When the craft arrives, the night is dark. No moon shines overhead. The craft travels around the world, taking humans from all over the Earth. The aliens send down a powerful channel of air, similar to a tunnel. It brings hundreds of people to the craft.

The aliens begin their work. They place the humans in suspended, tubular compartments. There are thousands of humans. The tubes are made of a transparent material similar to glass or plastic. Their bodies are naked and completely shaved. Wires run from the tubes to a main instrument, like a computer. The aliens study them for a while.

On the planet Earth, the leaders of government and science are somewhat confused and unable to function mentally. Their thought process is in disarray. Some countries, such as the United States and Russia, are building a military power and weapons for self defense. That creation comes from the aliens. They intend it to do evil. The aliens are directing the humans to the twenty-first century and to the beginning of the end starting in 2012. At this time the phenomenon will occur. Humans will not see what will take place. It will be a slow-moving terror. The aliens have set the stage for the end of the human race.

After the test of the humans is finished, the aliens place them in different parts of the planet. These humans are designed to bring havoc and terror to the human race.

The aliens travel back to the year 1835 for the exploration of fuel. The aliens need oil to help produce the material necessary for humans to advance and develop new machines for the future, taking them to the point of space travel and self-devastation.

The more people make, the more they want. They become obsessed with space exploration, seeking new planets and new source of life in outer space. All kinds of new energy are developed. Aircraft and spaceships are also in order to go where humans have never gone before. They want to go even farther into the boundless Universe. They dream that it will come true. They believe that machines and robotics are the answer to taking care of the problems of human society. Yes, the mind of man develops in a rapid way. Electronics and chips, small as the head of a pin, make it possible to move toward humanity's goal of incorporating better things into human life.

Slowly, humans forget where they came from and who they are.

In medicine, they also advance rapidly, ten times per year. By 2012, healing is very advanced. Every time humans contract a new disease, they fight back and develop new miracle drugs for their salvation. Humans work hard for a new exploration in creating new ideas and imagination. They escalate to more successful creations: better aircraft, automobiles, homes, living commodities, and foods. They become spoiled and unreasonable in all things.

Space travel begins in the late 1960s with unmanned missiles. They test with animals first and finally humans in space. All is done with the instruction of the aliens, step by step. In 1969, the first human set foot on the Moon.

"We will build stations on the Moon. We will colonize it with people. Many great accomplishments are in our future," the president declares to the citizens of America and the world.

Humans always come up empty-handed, to this day and beyond.

The aliens have men in check, under control. They implant ideas into people's craniums. They will return in a hundred years.

The beginning of a new project, a process of genetic engineering, starts in 1935 in Germany. A transformation takes place there. This evil plan has been planted in their minds by the aliens.

Cloning

This new project is the cloning of humans.

But it is not the time that the aliens chose for completion. That is only the beginning. It comes to fruition in 2012. That is the year that the first human experiment for cloning begins. The first clone does not survive. The scientists and doctors know the lab is not adequate for human cells and DNA testing. It is insufficient for experimentation and the development of human cloning. They are unsuccessful in engaging the process of living tissue, so they begin using animals. In time, they get what they want.

In the meantime, the world governments create a forum of experts in the fields of science, chemistry, engineering, mathematics, mechanics and medicine. They call it the S.S.D.O.C. (Space Scientific Development Organism Cloning).

The human race is in constant disarray. Wars, famine, disorder of governments, the accumulation of laws to constrain peoples' lives from freedom. It becomes a terrible place to be. By the summer of 2012, many terrible things occur: climate change, the economy, unemployment, and inflation. Oil prices rocket to $210 a barrel, and humanity's task of making things better becomes harder and harder. But they still are spending money to develop new technology. The year of a big change has come, from developing new machines to greater space ship. The space shuttle is a thing of the past. With a new spacecraft and the capability of going faster and farther, it was time to establish the new laboratory for the beginning of a successful experiment to create a better human, the S.U. (super human). The spaceship is called the Arc. It is the size of a football field, one hundred feet high, with many compartment used for many other experiments. The first spaceship of this type is named *Adam*.

In 2013, the ship departs from Earth, carrying the greatest and purest DNA from the best humans in the history of the race. After a successful take off, communications between mission control on Earth and *Adam* are crystal clear. They get ready for the second spaceship. It takes about six months. This one they call *Eve*. It is the mother ship, larger than *Adam*, with different organism, cells, microbes, bacteria, and DNA from plants, bugs, insects, mammals, amphibians, and humans. It is spectacular. Now the human race is up again with hope beyond belief.

"Things will get better now," they say. But they don't know the outcome of all this, that it is all for evil to the human race and the Earth.

On Earth, things go well for a short time, but this time of tranquility and happiness comes to an end with a terrorist attack, a bomb detonated in the center of Tel Aviv. The explosion is large, with more than five thousand people dead and thousands injured. Chaos, panic, and destruction. The hope for peace is over. For the next days and months, problems continue to arise: more deaths and new diseases. The bomb is made to kill and wreak havoc in Israel with chemical properties to destroy the country. The poison from the explosion gets into the air and the water. It contains major new types of bacteria, with no known cure. Within the Israeli government, panic occurs. They claim that the attack comes from Iran. The councilor and the leaders organize an air strike against Iran. But before they can attack they need the United Nations' advice to avoid mistakes. An investigation takes place to find the ones who caused this terror, to determine which country is involved. The UN security council comprises the United States, Canada, Italy, Britain, France, Germany, and Australia. These countries will make the final decision on when and where to strike.

For the human race, the situation goes from bad to terrible. The problem now is not just man-made disasters with bombs and chemicals, but also natural disasters: tornados, hurricanes, tsunamis, earthquakes, volcanoes, and—on top of it all—the economy is in shambles. Markets are falling, the world is in turmoil, and countries fight against one other in revolutions, civil wars, and coups d'état. The lack of jobs and the explosive population growth is so great that the planet cannot support it. The leaders of world governments need to work fast to develop new means of survival before it is too late.

Years go by, but all attempts are futile. Instead of making new jobs in agriculture, they create jobs to make missiles, spaceships, and bombs. The decision is to go out into the Universe and explore new galaxies and new planets, to find a better place for humanity to live. This is nothing but a dream, an illusion brought on by human curiosity. They are not capable of bettering themselves. Their brains are programmed by the aliens. They will not go anywhere. Their capabilities become stagnate. Communication with *Adam* and *Eve* becomes less and less frequent. They send another spaceship to investigate. This craft is called *Reportus 1*, but during launch everything goes wrong. With a terrifying explosion, thirty astronauts die in the blink of an eye. The accident puts space research and traveling on hold for a while.

In the meantime in space, the experiment of human cloning is taking place. After a long and exhaustive process, the first clone is created. By the following year, there were one hundred of them, male and female, equally the same. They are beautiful, tall, and intelligent. They name the male Primo and the female Prima, meaning the first clones created.

On Earth, the population is going mad. There is no place to go, food and water are scarce, water and air are becoming contaminated. They are dirty, hungry, and dismayed. China is becoming aggressive towards the West.

They have nothing to say except to blame. "All of the troubles of the world are caused by those from the Western hemisphere."

So there comes a time when the Chinese government throws out all westerners from the country. They return to Europe where they belong. People of European descent depart from all over the world to return to Europe.

In the meantime, aggression and hunger for power devastates Africa with civil wars. Major climate disasters signal the end of Africa and its people. For them, it is the end of the world. Millions of people die every day until just a few animals remain, but even they slowly die. Africa is a desert land with dead bodies, a dead continent. After the Europeans move from Africa, all hell breaks loose. The Africans have no means of taking care of themselves and the land in the face of climate change. It is the beginning of the end, their doomsday.

Six months to the day, the UN comes up with the answer. They concluded that two countries were involved in the Tel Aviv attack: Syria and Iran. They coordinated the attack and the making of the bomb.

The UN meets with the Israeli parliament for a solution, deciding on the best attack on those two states. The Israelis decide to attack.

"We will strike by night and by air. The strike will take place at midnight on December 25, 2013."

In Iran at that time, they are relaxed, with very little fear of an attack from anyone. The same attitude prevails in Syria. They are tranquil, not worried about an attack. Four American super stealth bombers depart from Israel on the bombing mission. In a surprise attack, the Israelis drop two MC-1 nuclear bombs. These old bombs were converted to be nuclear devices for more destruction. The next day, the news reports that Iran lost all military capability. About five hundred thousand people were dead and over a million injured. The fate of Syria was even more terrifying: nearly one million dead and two million injured. The state was destroyed. A terrible smell of chemicals hung in the air. No country was there to help.

Now China is angry because of the westerner's use of nuclear terror. They call upon India for a meeting of experts to organize a comprehensive way of dealing with this matter. At the meeting are also Japan and North Korea. They come up with many ways to deal with the Westerners. The prime minister of China is the head of organizing the complex idea to exterminate the evil white man.

"For many, many years, this race has been controlling the planet. For most of the world, it seems to be the white man's law and way of life! We have to end this with a surprise attack."

"Not yet," the Russian prime minister says. "We need to examine all solutions before starting the third World War."

Russia at this time is coordinating stability in its own country. The situation there is also in shambles. The economy, lack of work, and depression cause rebellion and civil war. Most of the country has no electric power or water. Death is everywhere and communication with the rest of the world is sporadic. The only things that the Russians have are nuclear missile silos and rusty equipment. Their means of transportation is ninety percent dead. Food is also scarce. They kill, loot, and destroy anything and everything. They cut most of the trees for fire so they can be warm.

Some of them travel to the western parts of Europe. These people are children of European descent.

In space, the two spacecraft slowly move from the Earth's atmosphere, separating from all Earth communications. The dream for the superhuman begins at a distance from reality.

Humanity is trying to find solutions for a positive outlook at life, but after searching for answers, they came back with empty hands. The EU and the US look for some alternative to save the world and the human race from its end. Many people become religious and pray for salvation. Others believe that aliens will come and take them. But all is in vain; no aliens, no gods in sight, just destructive disasters all around the Earth. It looks like the end of the world.

Scientists from the EU and US find themselves in the midst of confusion, with little to no ideas. They study and study day and night for months. They use all they have, going back thousands of years, looking for answers. They find none.

The Dream

They restudy Egyptian and Roman literature, as well as history and science, all with little results. One day a professor of mathematics is strolling through a field in England when he comes across a crop sign. With curiosity, he looks and notices something different about this crop circle. After the discovery of early crop circles when people wanted to know the significance of these signs, scientists had stopped investigating them because too many turned out to be hoaxes.

He needs to work hard, because he has discovered something new. This one is different from all the others.

"Something is strange about this sign … it is calling me … I feel I need to stay here and study until I find what it is that is trying to tell me!"

After a few days without progress, he gives up and calls upon his colleagues to study this new phenomenon.

"Why now?"

A professor of chemistry and a geologist join him. They go to the area and began to work, hoping to find the answer as soon as possible.

The new crop circle is very hard to solve. The professors decide to take a plane to study this new design from the air. Once they reach an appropriate altitude, they observed clearly that the sign is very different from all the others.

The crop circle takes the form of a large circle inside of a large triangle. The triangle and circle are nested inside a square. The square, triangle, and circle are set inside a larger circle with gears. On every gear is a smaller circle with a gear, and on each of those small gears are many gears. Then they see a face that resembles the face of an Egyptian, Aztec, Mayan, Asian, and African in the center of the circle.

They are very confused by the design. They see all of that but understand nothing.

"This is crazy. What is the meaning of this?"

So after an hour and hundreds of pictures, they decide to go back down on the ground and investigate the interior of the sign.

"We will take more samples and pictures, and then study them in a laboratory for information. We will see if all of this makes sense."

Going back to the year 1970 to see if there were any clues, they find pictures of all the signs from the 70s. They put them together with this most recent sign. They work for a week, day and night, on the matter, hoping something good would surface for the good of the planet and the human race.

In space now, the spacecraft have lost communication with the space center on Earth. No one knows what is going on there and what is happing to them.

In the spacecraft *Eve*, the scientists are conducting wild experiments in cloning, with different DNA from microbes and cells, mixing and matching all kind of genetic material to create new species for the betterment of human life. They engage in a new way of using chemistry and genetic engineering.

The first creation is a plant they called CPC (cloning plant cell). With natural and artificial chemicals, they develop a new nucleonic man-made plant. It produced a new synthetic molecule that will help speed the cloning process. From that, they move on to insects, reptiles, and mammals.

The characteristics and quantity of these new clones surpass their expectations. They begin cloning and testing with insects. They are playing gods. They mix cells and DNA from all types to create new species of ants, butterflies, reptiles, birds, fish, and all forms of mammals.

Their attempt at cloning is successful.

"Very good, colleagues and friends. We are on the right path. We will modify all that we have done and progressively we will create new creatures and develop a new way of life for our society."

The scientists on the spacecrafts celebrate their monumental accomplishments. But they don't have a clue what's going on back on the planet Earth. The turmoil of wars and chaos is taking a toll on the human race.

Six months go by. The good professor who discovered the crop circle insists on an answer. He believes the new sign is a message from outer space to instruct and direct humanity for the future. He feels he needs to revisit the circle and find the answer there.

After five hours there, the answer is clear him. He knows that this time there is no mistake. He feels good about the whole thing and needs to see his colleagues. With their study, they can prove that the answer is right, so they can face the EU emperor to present this new information. Their hope is that the world can go to work with renewed energy and have a great perspective on society as a whole.

From all the information given by the professors, the kingdom of EU acknowledges that it will be good for the world. Soon they commence building new factories so people can work. They build new equipment with new designs. These new items will help the world to move toward a new future again with knowledge and health and prosperity.

"The human race shall be as great again as it was during the Romans period," they all agree with gladness. Joy is in the air.

They set a new forum to coordinate the future, a mandate for the world to be united as one and to go fourth and began a new world. The EU emperor notified some other countries, such as the United States, Canada, and Australia. These countries are sisters of Europe. They send a message to China also, so they can work with all Asia. But something goes wrong. China refuses the deal. They feel under attack again by Westerners and their control of the world.

"No, no, no, no! We will never be the same or work together!"

The Chinese prime minister is enraged. He calls upon India again for a meeting so they could organize the same movement as the Europeans.

Another six months pass. Europe and the united countries began constructing the new world. It is going well and moving quickly. Everything is going smoothly. The progress of this new knowledge opens more venues for grander accomplishments.

One night in August 2014, a terrible earthquake measuring 9.1 on the Richter scale hits Texas, killing over six million people and injuring twelve million. The whole state was destroyed. In Mexico, New Mexico, Oklahoma, Louisiana, and Arkansas, devastation and death are everywhere. The country is in a terrible state. Help arrives there slowly. More and more people die. For them, it is just the beginning; the tremors continue for days. They have no water, food, or medical supplies. Communication with the rest of the country is cut off. News is obtained only by plane and helicopter.

The sister countries Canada and Australia, along with Europe, send planes to the area to deliver water, food, and medical emergency supplies, along with new types of equipment created with the new knowledge they had obtained.

In the meantime, China celebrates the devastation of America. "They deserve this, and now is the time to get them for what they have done to Iran and Syria! The time is now!"

So they push a button and launch ten nuclear missiles aimed toward the United States and its cities. These missiles do not have the same shape as the old kind. These are a new design, similar to airplanes. The US and Canada detect the missiles via their Space Guard Optical Site (S.G.O.S). They intercept the incoming missiles with their antiballistic missiles and disintegrate them in space. But three of the Chinese missiles get through. They descend on three American cities: New York, Philadelphia, and San Francisco, simultaneously killing over fifty million people and injuring about the same. The destruction is beyond imagination; it is unthinkable.

In desperation the president of the United States exclaims, "Why attack after all of this? How can we continue living? It is over for us!"

China's prime minister sent a message to US to walk away from the European alliance and live. Otherwise, the consequence will be the destruction of America. The United States sends a distress call to the EU for answers.

"Please tell us what we should do!!"

The EU emperor goes to America to visit. He explains to the president a strategy, and then leaves the country. He leaves all the equipment and supplies there. For the next few years, China controls the United States and all of South America, using them like slaves. They also appointed a new president, a man of Chinese-American descent. His name is Carl Chiin-Gu.

In the few months, the EU advances greatly in their defensive and protective technology. They develop a continent with a superior way of life. People of European descent return to their place of birth, millions upon millions.

After the Chinese take over the Americas, they figure that now is the time to spy on the EU to see what is going on there. The Chinese don't have a clue about the EU and what is happening over there. The president calls a small meeting with the most prestigious people in the new government.

"What would be the best way to find out what the situation is in the EU? They are quiet. I would like to know what is taking place there!"

One of their most notorious spies exclaims, "If you send a spy there to investigate, he would have to be white. Right now, you don't have many to choose from. The old CIA and FBI are dismantled. You, sir, need to form a new one with white people if you want to infiltrate the EU."

The president is informed that Canada and Australia were doing well, similar to the EU.

He formulates his plan. "The best way for now is to form this new organization and send a spy right away!"

Utopiaromana

They find a few willing white men to do the job. They believe it will be good for the country. They promise the president that they will collect all the information needed and come back to report. At a time when a multitude of Americans are immigrating to Canada, President Carl Chiin-Gu see the opportunity to send his spies with the crowd. There are ten of them.

The spies arrive in Canada and pass the border, just because they were white. No other races were welcome there. That is a change taking place in Canada. The situation is the same for Australia, which receives immigrants from South Africa, boats full of white people. In Europe, too, immigration comes from the East.

From Canada an aircraft departs to the EU with eight of the spies on board. They arrive in Europe and begin searching for clues and information. When they arrive in the EU, they look around and are stupefied by what they see. After they go all over the EU, six of them remain there and two depart to Australia. There, conditions are also the same as in the EU. After a few months, one of the spies jumps on board an aircraft to Canada and returns to America to deliver the news and information.

He meets with the president to report everything.

"It was beautiful. People were happy and joyful. Everywhere, everything was clean, like crystal. There were shops and restaurants, new construction and new cities. There was music, free food and drinks for all the people, and no police or soldiers to be seen."

The president asks, "Is there no law there? Are they free to do anything they want?"

The spy continues, "Transportation is different than we know."

"What are you saying? How is it different?" the president questions.

"It is from new advances in technology and design. They use different materials than what we know and used in the past. But I did not find the information I was looking for."

So again, the question is raised, "Is anything you collected helpful to us?"

"The only thing I noticed was that the famous crop sign was everywhere. It was carved on streets and building. It was very peculiar."

They look at him confused. They don't believe what they hear.

"I did not understand. They don't call it Europe anymore. The new name is Utopiaromana."

The spy continues, "So, here I am with empty hands."

The spy is conversing with the president with sadness and great sorrow, because he had returned to America.

Europe had turned out to be a perfect country and a peaceful one, with advanced people."

"With care and love for one another, they all kept the streets, their homes, and the country in perfect condition."

President Carl Chiin-Gu is furious and confused by the information given to him by the spy.

"What are you saying? Signs? Crop signs? It is nothing more than an old bogus and ridiculous manifestation of man-made things. Off with these; they are not of importance to me."

The meeting comes to an end.

In space, on the craft *Eve*, something is going wrong. The genetic engineers are successful in cloning. They too, create a human clone. This clone is different from the one made in *Adam*. This one is made of different human DNA and cell types. It includes genetic material from all races mixed together. This cell looks perfect. After the first clone is created, the process develops quickly. After one year, there are three hundred sixty-six clones, both male and female. The first male clone was named Me, for the female was Ma. These clones are smaller than their counterparts from *Adam*. They are short in stature, with evil minds.

The clones take control of the craft and depart into space toward the Moon. They remain there for about a year, with no communication from Earth or from the spacecraft *Adam*. The separation will erase all memory of their history. They will not know each other for a long time.

The prime minister of China becomes aware of the news from President Carl Chiin-Gu. He orders all the scientists to meet and discuss the situation, including everything that the spy, Mr. Fury, collected on his trip.

They need to find a solution very soon. They press him for more information.

"There is nothing more to say. The only thing that comes to my mind is the design of the sign, the crop circle." o

All the information is reported to the leaders. They advise them quickly to send another spy with Mr. Fury.

"We believe the signs have a message for our future."

China, America, and South America are in bad shape in agriculture, jobs, and their economy. Provisions like food and water are becoming scarce. In the US, other disasters develop. At two in the afternoon, an earthquake began to rumble in California. The Santa Andreas fault was slipping. Slowly, the ground was moving, cutting with terrible deep grooves, separating chunks of land. All around the state, it causes a change in the landscape. Some areas fall into the ocean, taking everything on it. The existence of California disappears for good.

All the remains from the nuclear bomb that was sent by China prior to the earthquake disappear into the ocean. The country is devastated. Chaos is everywhere. It is a terrible place to be. The states around California also suffer major consequences with more earthquakes and apocalyptic disasters, death beyond any human imagination. In Texas, turmoil and draught are killing the rest of the people, and Texas is becoming a desert and a horrible place. In the neighboring states there are also death and diseases, no water or food, and help iss slow to come.

The prime minister of China and the president of America send the two spies to collect information from Europe, now Utopiaromana, so they can change their countries to be like them.

The spies get dropped off at the Canadian border to board a ship to Europe. When they arrive there and stand in line at a checkpoint, Mr. Fury sees that something has changed. There are guards everywhere.

"This is different. The guards are new. We need to stay calm. I will speak to him."

The guard is checking all the passengers one-by-one in an unusual way. He only looks at their right arms.

Then it is the spies' turn.

"Good day, citizens!"

"Good day, sir!"

"Can you please uncover your wrist and show me your mark?"

The spies look at each other. Surprised and confused they ask, "May we ask, sir, what it is you are looking for?"

The guard gently replies, "The mark. Your citizen mark."

Mr. Fury didn't know that in Utopiaromana many laws and regulations have changed. It is very hard to infiltrate the new nation. Now all citizens of Utopiaromana have a code on the right wrist for security purposes. It also signifies that they are free to enter any Utopiaromana countries.

The guards take them. They place them in a special room to question them about their voyage.

One month has passed since they left America. The president and the prime minister are worried about the outcome. Now they find themselves in a jam.

"If they know that we send spies there, we will have some explaining to do, just in case the emperor questions us," the president says.

The prime minister replies, "Don't worry. I have a plan that it is going to make everything better for us, for our countries, and for our people."

"And what that will be?" the president asks with distress.

"Utopiaromana will be under our watchful eye. We will be monitoring from space with a new optical scope. We will see any movements they make."

President Carl Chiin-Gu is not sure of that.

Then the bad news comes from Canada.

"Warning: anyone that sends spies to Utopiaromana will pay the consequences with complete annihilation."

The nations that are together with China and America gather in China to discuss the matter and develop a secure plan with a defensive program against Utopiaromana.

Then the American president says, "Gentlemen, I will call the emperor and apologize to him. I will ask him to forgive our mistake."

They all agree, and so the president communicates with the emperor. "Honorable Emperor, please accept our apologies. We will not infiltrate your kingdom again. It was an act of bad faith on our part!"

Emperor Luscious Fortes Caesar personally replies. "For now, Utopiaromana will dismiss all acts by your allies.

For the future, I place full responsibility on you for anyone taking any action against us. We will attack without warning, first against America, and then against China. Spread this warning to all of your allies."

The communication is cut off.

A year later, hell breaks loose. In America, China, India, and the Middle East, many situations occur. One of them is the shutdown of oil refineries. The economy is out of control. Dark days are upon them. In their poverty, the small amount of sustainable supplies diminish every hour. The dead and sick are everywhere. Hospitals are full. The water supply is low. There is not enough for everyone. Desperation causes civil wars and revolutions. Murder and theft are now the way of life.

China's government is building more weapons, from airplanes to tanks and nuclear bombs. It now has the largest army in the world, ten times the size of Utopiaromana. The military comprises more than six million soldiers.

Two million soldiers are sent from China to the Middle East to establish order and control. One million go to India. Two million are stationed in the Americas. A million remain in Asia.

The most important army camps are in Africa and the Middle East, so they can observe Utopiaromana, just in case of an attack.

In the meantime, China and America are expanding their knowledge, creating new technology, making stronger and more powerful bombs. They think that building this so-called "innovative technology" will make the world bow to them, and they will be the only empire to control the whole Universe.

Again they are deluding themselves. The consequences are grave, just as they were with the Egyptians and the Mayans, whom the aliens exterminated. That was the reason the aliens come: for vengeance, to make humanity pay for their stupidity and bad decisions, and for playing god. The payment is terror, horror, panic, chaos, and death. This is humanity's gift from the others, the aliens.

It is a game for the aliens. They can do anything they want to people and animals.

The Beginning & The End

Beginning in 2011, the aliens return. They are watching the human's activity and progress. After they examine the planet, the decision is made to give humanity knowledge of the precise time of its end.

"The countdown will commence at midnight on 1.1.2012. It ends at midnight on 12.30.2040, exactly 245,280 hours human time. That is the time for the extermination and the end of this race."

In 2018, America and China have a conference. They reach an agreement to a talk with the emperor of Utopiaromana, in regards to their power and ability to destroy Utopiaromana, along with its allies, Canada and Australia.

President Carl Chiin-Gu calls the emperor.

"Honorable Emperor Luscious, I have some news of great importance. I am suggesting that you and your empire pay careful attention to this information. It will be given to you only once."

The emperor with tranquility and confidence in his empire replies, "Important news? Of what? I clearly said that dialog between our nations was over. Isn't that correct?"

President Carl Chiin-Gu responds angrily, "Emperor, sir, you don't understand the consequences! If we cannot come together in accord, I will not be responsible for the consequences for your empire and the citizens of Utopiaromana."

The moment arrives, and the sign for which the emperor was waiting comes. With that, he cuts off all communication for good. That is the end of any relationship with the outside world.

The turmoil and panic in America gets worse. Violence rages. Chaos is pandemic. The government takes action, imposing a curfew and a new form of laws.

In South America, Asia, India, and the Middle East, terror consumes the populous with famine and pestilence. The pandemic continues. No one knows what is going on.

"It is the end of society! We are all going to die!"

People scream in panic and horror. They shout from the bottom of their lungs, "God is punishing the world and the human race".

The dead are everywhere, piles and piles of bodies. The smell of burnt flesh from humans and beasts alike filled the air.

In Utopiaromana, all is good and peaceful. The emperor calls upon Australia and Canada to organize transportation for all the citizens to get ready to move to Utopiaromana to their new home.

"We will be one, in one land. We will not make the same mistake that the Romans made. We will stay together."

By the year 2020, Canada and Australia have transported most of their people with the new spacecraft that the engineers of Utopiaromana created. It is fast and large, with a capacity of 12,000 people at one time.

From Australia to the empire, the trip took only one hour; from Canada, twenty-four minutes.

Utopiaromana is a place of security with an impenetrable electrical wall circling all its lands and oceans, for kilometer upon kilometer, protecting Europe from intruders. There is no way to get in. In space, satellites observe the whole planet.

In the meantime, America is searching for the best archeologist. They want to find new possibilities and signs that they may have missed in the past. So now the president, Carl Chiin-Gu, has access to all the countries with the help of China's prime minister. They have a free passage to Africa and all Asia, ripe for new explorations. The archeologists and astronomers travel toward the southeast of Mexico. They arrive at an unknown island. They know little of the history of the island and its people. They survey and find no a place to enter. After they rendezvous, they contact the president to inform him and to ask for a decision on what to do.

President Carl Chiin-Gu replies, "Did you find anything?"

"Yes. We saw a wall around the island, a very tall wall, about 100 meters. The surface is smooth and the cut is perfect."

"Well, that is different. Maybe something will transpire. I will send a helicopter so you can get in and survey the island. You will have sufficient supplies to remain there until you find something that will help our world and our people."

They reside there for a few weeks, searching for clues and signs. They come up empty. They decide to stay there until they find something of any kind. In the Americas the pandemic is vast and out of control with diseases and natural disasters. The government was losing control of the people.

President Carl Chiin-Gu places a curfew on all citizens.

"Those who don't obey will be shot on the spot with no mercy."

Angry and out-of-control people take the law as a joke. They become aggressive and more violent toward one other. Revolution is on the rise. Killing and starvation wreaks havoc on the land.

It is the same fate for Asia and Africa, with millions of people dying. The world of the human race is coming to an end.

There is no answer to the problem. Leaders take extreme measures. The decision is to use force against the populous. In a different way in Utopiaromana, all is well. There are no complications there or in Canada or Australia. The manifestation of tranquility is beyond anyone's imagination. Outsiders have no idea on what is going on inside of Utopiaromana, and the insiders don't know the atrocities of the rest of the world.

Two months pass. On the island, the archeologists come across a square pillar of stone. It looks similar to granite or marble. It is smooth and brilliant, measuring 6 meters high, 6 meters wide, and 6 meters deep. On the top is a hole 66.6 centimeters across. From the top of the pillar to the center of the hole is 2 meters. From the sides to the center of the hole is 3 meters. From the bottom to the center hole is 4 meters.

On the stone are symbols that resemble Egyptian and Mayan writing. The scholars have a hard time translating the stone. They work night and day with no conclusion. They send a message to the president to send everything they can find on Egyptian and Mayan history and language. The president sends all material he can get his hands on. After they receive them, they get to work on it rapidly. They don't want to waste any time on this amazing discovery. Forty-two days go by. Finally they find something significant. There is no doubt that the translation is correct. It is verified by multiple scholars. As much as they might want it to be otherwise, there is no denying the message on the stone.

This pillar is perfectly symmetrical, calculated from the Universe Planetary. Once the hole is in line with the planets and the Moon, it will begin the chain reaction that will eliminate planet Earth and its atmosphere. It will be a dramatic evolution with disasters. This is the key of knowledge, to measure time and dimension for the future of humanity and its end. The countdown for the end of humans and all living creatures will commence on day 730,000 from day 0. The chaos, confusion, and multiple natural disasters leading to the end of the Earth and humanity shall commence on day 14,600 at 0 hour.

They stop reading, trembling and scared. They decide to go back home to meet the president and to confide in him the importance of that translated news.

Meanwhile in space, the spacecraft *Eve* is far into space. There is no trace of spacecraft *Adam*, and most satellites are destroyed or lost in the dark waste of the Universe. On Earth, the bad news reaches the president, who doesn't take the news very well.

"So this is all you understand? How real and serious is it? Is the translation accurate or do you need more time to excavate new material? Now that we have this information, how can we use it for the salvation of the human race?"

With sadness, the professors look at one other and exclaim, "We are very sorry. That is all we have. The calculations are right, and the countdown has already begun. We do not have time to waste. You need to share this information with the world."

President Carl Chiin-Gu, horrified, sends the news through all the Americas. The chaos continues. Death is increasing, and there is little to no food. Hesitant, he sends the news to Emperor Luscious Fortes Caesar.

The emperor reopens communications with the president once more.

"I received the information. How did you get it, Mr. President? And how do I know that it is serious and not some despicable trick?"

The president replies, "It is not a trick, honorable Emperor! The information comes from the archeologists and anthropologist. They collected it from the monolith, which had an inscription in the ancient languages of the Egyptians and Mayans, as well as another language unknown to us."

The emperor remains silent for a while then he replies, "I will give you five minutes to convince me that this is all true."

So the president begins to tell the emperor everything he knows from the professors. Then he pauses for few seconds.

"Do you believe me? Our world has very little time. We need to work together on this. Every country needs to be united. They need to send their most intelligent people in all fields to come up with some ideas, to create a safety net, for the masses and the planet."

"This is an amazing discovery, the island and the granite! But I don't see any proof of this information," replies the emperor. "Again, I have to ask, when will the end of the world occur?"

"The countdown began back in the year 2000. But the stone has confirmed 2012 with a remaining time of 14.000 days."

The emperor replies skeptically. "What predictions do you and the professors have for the end of the world and human society?"

Destruction

The president choses his words carefully. "Most of the destruction will be caused by the planet itself."

The emperor replies, "With earthquakes, tornados, tsunamis, and droughts? A meteor? Or perhaps nuclear devastation by you and your ally, China?"

"No, no! Not from us," the president replies, "but from the Earth itself. We can't determine exactly how it will occur, but the meaning of the monolith is quite clear."

The emperor looks out from his balcony. He sees the beautiful shinning capital of Utopiaromana and remains unconvinced that all of that would come to an end.

"Did your professors come up with an estimation of when?"

"Yes, they did," the president replies. "According to information from the Earth clock of the Egyptians and the Mayans coupled with the newly discovered pillar, the calculated time appears to be in year 6000 in the 6th month on the 6th day.

"What hour of the day will the first disaster will take place?"

After a few seconds pause, the president replies, "Regretfully, we don't know the hour."

In a few words, the emperor says, "I will reflect on this information seriously. Thank you, Mr. President."

Time passes. The Earth's temperature begins to change. A large earthquake rattles India at magnitude 9.2 for 7 minutes, destroying 70 percent of the capital city of Mumbai. Over nine million people die, and the remaining 4 –5 million are injured and scattered all over the land. The devastation is beyond repair and the death toll continues to rise for days.

In Africa, the temperature is not normal, rising from 40 to 50 degrees Celsius. A multitude of problems prolongs the dry weather, starting a drought in central Africa that has a ripple effect. It expands all over the continent, killing everything: people, animals, and plants. Lakes and rivers dry up. A dust clouds engulfs the land. There is no place to run, only a place to expire. In Utopiaromana, the emperor meets with heads of state to discuss the information he received from the American president during the conversation.

One of the heads of state exclaims, "We don't need to take action on this! It could be another trick, so they can infiltrate and damage our utopia."

The emperor decides to take a vote on what to do with the information. The vote is unanimous not to do anything. Luscious Fortes Caesar calls Mr. Carl Chiin-Gu and delivers the answer from the people of Utopiaromana not to go forth and change for the rest of the world and its problems.

"We will remain neutral in this matter for now."

"Emperor, you and your people are making a grand error in not joining us. You will regret it. We are all going to need immense help from each other. Please, please convince them," he screams with horror.

The emperor says goodbye and closes communication.

At the North and South Poles, the climate is also making dramatic changes. After the earthquake in India, the Earth's axis shifted by five centimeters, moving the Earth closer to the sun. The temperature is getting warmer, and the glaciers are melting fast.

North/South Pole

The North Pole, also known as the Geographic North Pole or Terrestrial North Pole, is the point in the northern hemisphere where the Earth's axis of rotation meets the Earth surface. The North Pole is the northernmost point on Earth, lying diametrically opposite the South Pole. It defines geodetic latitude 90 degrees north as well as the direction of True North. At the North Pole, all directions point south; all lines of longitude converge there, so its longitude can be defined in any degree value. While the South Pole lies on a continental landmass, the North Pole is located in the middle of the Arctic Ocean amidst waters that are permanently covered with constantly shifting sea ice.

Glaciers

Glaciers are large, persistent bodies of ice. Originating on land, a glacier flows slowly due to stress induced by its weight. The crevasses and other distinguishing features of a glacier are due to its flow. Another consequence of glacial flow is the transportation of rock and debris scooped up from its substrate. It sculpts the land as it moves, leaving landforms like cirques and moraines. A glacier forms when the accumulation of snow and sleet exceeds the amount of snow that melts. Over many years, a glacier will eventually form as the snow compacts and turns to ice. A glacier is distinct from sea ice and lake ice that form on the surface of bodies of water.

The word *glacier* comes from the Latin (*glacia*).

The Moon also has stress changes. It moves more slowly. It is only a few seconds difference, but it is more than enough to disrupt the Earth's atmosphere and rotation. The result of this change destabilizes the Earth. Its rotation takes on a wiggling motion and speeds up by half minute per day.

In Utopiaromana at this point, they live well. There are no problems or disasters. They believe that the protective electric dome will keep them from harm's way. The emperor knows everything about what is going on outside. Through his satellites, he is aware of the changes affecting the Earth and Moon, as well as all the chaos all over the planet, but he chooses not to intervene or help. 185 days after India's earthquake, a chain reaction of tremors takes place around the world. An 8.9 quake strikes the Americas, Mexico, and South America. Two-thirds of all living things are destroyed. The quake causes a tsunami with waves over 35 meters in height. It reaches Australia. Most of the natives are underwater. Many other islands in that region suffer the same fate. From Texas to Florida, about 180 kilometers of coastal land are also underwater, and millions are dead. Panic and terror are everywhere. There is no escape from the destruction. The end for the human race is near and no one can change the course that the Aliens designed for the punishment of humanity.

SOS Into Space

They pray and pray to all gods and aliens to rescue them from the end of the world. China is also panicking. With all that is going on in the world, the prime minister and leaders meet.

"The emperor is not taking action to help humanity. The white man just cares for his own race. We need to take action against him and his mighty Utopiaromana. The time is now; we have the arsenal to damage his protected country, Canada. Maybe then he will wake up and realize the consequences for his people."

The Chinese engage for the extermination of Canada with four nuclear bombs. Two of them are aimed at Utopiaromana. These are decoys dispatched from China. The other two are authentic weapons aimed at Canada. From space, satellites detect and intercept the two missiles aimed at Europe with a sonic vibration. They direct the missiles into space and destroy them. But it is too late for Canada. Two simultaneous explosions over the country bring destruction and death once more.

It is a world of chaos, terror, disbelief, and panic. For the first time, the people of Utopiaromana receive news of their sister country, which has been decimated by the Chinese. They are hungry for revenge.

The emperor calls upon the citizens for a decision on what action is to be taken.

"It will be done quietly and swiftly in a surprising manner," the emperor exclaims furiously. "And it will be a war without end."

The entire citizenry is in concord with the emperor. They go forth.

Two craft depart from Utopiaromana's universal craft base. These craft are designed to travel faster than the speed of sound. One is destined for Beijing; the other for North Africa, where China occupied the land long ago, establishing a mighty military base from which they hoped to control the world of Utopiaromana.

In the rest of the world, death from disasters, both natural and man-made, continues. Most of the nuclear reactors in the Americas are on the brink of meltdown. Terror and chaos live on.

The aliens return to the planet Earth. They have no need to come back, but they return once more anyway. There is nothing more to conquer. They get what they came for: the extraction of minerals and a horrific payment for the human race.

Who are they, these so-called aliens? And why do they come here? Where did they originate?

From above the Earth near the Moon, the Others are watching the humans, who are desperate for safety and salvation.

"Mission accomplished. We have conquered all. The

end is near for them and their planet. Earth will be a dead planet in the Universe. We will continue to search for a home, for a planet of our own."

So they depart into infinity.

The craft arrive at the precisely the same time. They drop five MC-1 nuclear bombs in China and two in North Africa. They completely destroy Beijing and decimate the Chinese military in Africa. Checkmate. The Chinese have no place to go but to suffer and die slowly. There is no help in sight. The American president Carl Chiin-Gu is horrified by the news he receives. He panics and is lost. He thinks that now Utopiaromana will attack his country. He tries to contact the emperor but without luck. All communications are out. He has no way of contacting the emperor. That is not all. The population is going crazy. There is terrorism, famine, and killing one another over what little food and water they have. And now they are marching towards the capital. The president barricades the capital with the military and a wall of spiked wire, so no one can get in or out. That way he feels safe.

With the nuclear reactors gone, the only electric machines are the ones running with oil.

The time of 0 hour is getting closer. The time remaining is 5,475 days.

In Myanmar China, a 9.7 earthquake erupts lasting 12 minutes. It occurs after the explosion of one of the bombs dropped from the craft. It is a 2000-kilo nuclear bomb designed to ensure devastation on the land and extermination of a race. A chain reaction takes place in Asia from the nuclear bombs, setting off earthquakes and a tsunami. It has a ripple effect that flows out to the whole world. Islands and beach fronts are underwater, changing the geographic map of the planet Earth and the course of the Earth's spin.

This change causes nature to make violent weather of an extraordinary magnitude in a disordered and disorganized way, from snow in Africa to meltdowns at the North and South Poles. The chain continues, causing eruptions of volcanoes all around the planet. The Utopiaromana satellites are the only witness of what is taking place. The emperor now feels that he is also responsible for causing this and now it is too late to do anything to save the Earth. The emperor manages to ready all spacecraft, loading them with thousands of people, including the military and all intelligent minds. The crafts are also filled with every kind of animal and plant from their utopia. It is too late for many living creature. The oceans are filled with dead fish and the land with all kind of animals and birds. Death is everywhere. There is terror and horror with no way to run and no place to hide. It is hell on Earth. In the past, Yellowstone National Park was a fantastic place to visit, but an explosion equal to 350 mega nuclear bombs eradicates the land. It is the eruption of a new volcano, sending ashes and lava into the sky. It is fatal to all living things. It creates a crater over 100 kilometers across. The eruption lasts for days and days.

The meltdown at the North and South Poles causes floods, destructions, and death. The population is dying, with no food and little water. For survival, they turn to cannibalism. Utopiaromana is in the edge of self-annihilation.

Turmoil begins to take its toll. The utopia that was is now hell. Darkness is upon them. Vesuvius also erupts, shooting black ashes and scorching stones the size of people's heads thousands of meters into the air. They fall down to Earth like meteors, killing people, plants, and animal. This goes on for weeks, destroying all of southern Italy northward past Florence. Everything is gone and dead. In central Utopiaromana, a tremendous explosion occurs in the mountains, affecting the land with an 8.1 magnitude earthquake. Everywhere there is destruction. The planet and the human race are doomed.

In the solar system, a change is taking place. The planets are moving into formation. The Earth's moon is transforming in color, turning red. It moves closer to the Earth. The sun grows larger and hotter. Earth's axis is disturbed. The planet is off its natural spin. It is the year 2035. The time remaining is 1,825 days. Two-thirds of all living organism are out of existence.

Praying For Salvation

Some of the surviving people believe that some kind of alien with a fantastic spaceship will arrive and save them from that nightmare. Others pray to God for mercy and salvation. All of that is nothing but empty feelings. It has no meaning. Chaos makes humans look for help in any direction and many places. The others, the aliens, are not in sight for now. They will not come back in the near future.

President Carl Chiin-Gu asks NASA for help. "Is anything we can do? Anything at all? We need to save people? Don't we have any space shuttles we can use?"

The answer is no.

"But we can send probes into space in search of someone out there. If there is someone, maybe they will understand our call for help. That is all we can do."

With distress and agony, the whole world is waiting for the end of the human race and the planet. It is the year 2038, 700 days before humanity ceases to exist. The planets slowly and in a systematic order get into formation in a straight line with each other. They await the final countdown for the end of planet Earth and all living things.

It is recorded that aliens had come and gone many times in human history. The people of Earth hope that maybe the aliens will come back to adjust the planet and make it better than before, a place for a new life and a new beginning with a purified population. Or maybe the aliens will take them to another planet. Their hope is in vain. It is only their wishes and imagination. In the meantime the Earth's magnetic field is getting weaker, becoming more penetrable to the sun's rays. Slowly the planet begins to get hotter. NASA continues sending probes and distress signals into space. They are not successful.

From afar, the aliens are watching the Earth. They congratulate themselves for their accomplishment in taking revenge for what the humans did to planet Earth and to them.

Why did the Aliens come to Earth? Who are they? The Aliens (the Others) are man-made, the result of humanity's extravagant imagination and desire to play god with nature. They are the result of experiment after experiment on plants, animals, and humans.

Let's go back into the past and find out the cause of everything. Let's look at the events that took place on the planet, at how the planet arrived at this situation, at the point of no return.

It is 1915, the time of the first major World War. Millions of people are dead. From that day on, there were more wars and the beginning of experiment, from medicine to machines, from science and astronomy to engineering and architecture. And, most important, the development of means for mimicking nature and duplicating its properties.

Human knowledge advanced without consequence. With no consequences resulting from the mishaps, humans continued with their new inventions and creations: new machines, electrical power, radio, telephones, satellites, and navigation instruments.

In the mid 1930s, new technologies evolved, from fast airplanes, watercraft, construction of bridges and dams, to transportation of all kinds. The mechanics of creation and inventions got into gear. By 1937 humans began to study and work in genetic engineering, cloning plants, animals, and the first human. The first human was not successful. They killed the experiment for the time being. In 1942, a new order surfaced the take over the world with force. With new weapons and long-range missiles, it was time for the most powerful country to advance and conquer the world. And so the Second World War began.

Bloodshed and destruction continued for a few years, and then a new power on Earth was unleashed: the atomic bomb. It was natural progression of all events that humans had to endure. People began to predict the extermination of the human race.

Moving to a new era with more advanced knowledge, we came to the year 1982. It was the age of electronics, space travel, new satellites, and telescopic lenses sent into space. Humans now had greater armies and more countries had the capability of making nuclear weapons. Humanity was on the road of no return.

Humans increased the study of DNA, the splitting of cells, and genetic engineering. Their newest accomplishment was the first successful clone. It was a cow in

Australia and a sheep in Scotland. They cloned a monkey and a bird as well, but after some time each died. The scientist continued with the study for a while. Finally, they successfully cloned a sheep again. The animal was fine. Then they cloned another, and another. Now they had 1000 clones. They moved on to run tests with cows. That too was successful. The human population did not know they were eating meat from clones and other man-made substances.

In 1981, the United States launched the first Space Shuttle. Its purpose was to help build a large space center where humans could work on new advanced technology in a sophisticated laboratory for the developing of great things for humanity. The projected on which they worked were government secrets. The public had no knowledge of them. After the attempt to send humans to the Moon failed, the United States decided to remain close to Earth's atmosphere and build large living quarters in a space center.

The citizens praised the government for taking the country to new heights, becoming the most advanced nation in the world. Late in 1990, however, something went wrong in the laboratory on the space station. They were forced to stop what they were doing to investigate the accident. That was the last communication from the space station. Earth received no information about what was happing there. It was as if it had disappeared into the Universe.

NASA sent a Space Shuttle to investigate. The mission could not locate the station or any debris from it. Six months later, NASA sent one more to investigate what occur there. Again they came back empty-handed. The public had no clue that the government was lying to the citizen once more. They said that everything was good, that everything was going according to plan.

NASA continued sending shuttles into orbit. In 2000, the United States and the European Union together organized a space exploration team to build a new space station. They also hoped to work together on cloning. This second purpose, however, was not revealed to the public.

Playing God

A new laboratory, much larger than the prior one was constructed. A few years passed and the EU launched a new style of craft that was very large and self-powered. Its only purpose was cloning. It was called *Adam*. After six months, the USA with the help of EU sent a second ship with the same purpose. They called this one *Eve*. One problem was that the USA did not consult with the EU on what to take for study on the ship. They carried human DNA, as well as that of animals, plants and microbes to advance their knowledge ahead of the EU. So the adventure began.

While the two ships were 100,000 kilometer from each other, their communication was frequent. They shared what was going on with their experiments in cloning. The official doctor from *Adam* was conversing with the lead doctor from *Eve* when all hell broke loose.

"What?!? What did you say? You are studying all kind of cells from humans, plants, animals, and such? That is wrong! It goes against the original plan and the agreement signed by the two countries. I tell you that it will lead to a mishap, a genetic drift, and the consequences will be grave."

That was the last conversation between the two space craft.

On *Adam*, the doctors worked very hard to create the best genetic clone. They drifted away from the Earth's atmosphere past the point of no return. They were far away from the Earth, but they could still see the beautiful blue planet. Slowly, they got control of the craft. It was too late to return back home to Earth. Everything inside *Adam* was good and safe. The first successful clone was born. The entire ship celebrated this creation.

The clone was in perfect physical condition, and its proportions were ideal. It was a male, tall and handsome with black hair and blue eyes. Developmentally, he was the equivalent of someone in their early 30s.

He stood upright in his incubation chamber. The doctor opened its glass door. The clone smiled and began to walk out with a slow pace.

The doctor said, "Hello. Are you feeling OK? Can you hear and understand me?"

"Yes, I can," the clone replied in a calm and soft voice. "And I feel fine."

"This is fantastic," the doctor exclaimed. "It worked with the right cells and DNA. We will create perfection for Earth and the human race".

From that moment on, the clone became part of their study, learning all he needed to know. The clone began to help them create more clones. The second clone was a female. She too was tall and beautiful with black hair and blue eyes. They then created ten males, then ten females, and so on. The clones and the scientists worked together to develop higher quality materials for their needs. The crew at first was 500 men and women, and the craft's capability was 1000. The plan was to create one male and one female clone, and then return to Earth to continue their work and experiment with development in a gravity environment verses the non-gravity environment of the ship. But the situation changed after the craft was launched. Now they were about 1.5 million kilometers away from Earth. When they opened the visor and looked out from the window, they could see planet Earth engulfed in flames.

With sadness and tears on their eyes the doctors cried, "Goodbye, Mother Earth. Goodbye. Goodbye."

Take Over

Two million miles from *Adam* and traveling at high velocity, *Eve* was having trouble with their new creations. They cloned a mismatch of DNA, including cells from microbes, plants, and animals. This caused mutations in the genes. Some of the clones were strange specimens. These were destroyed or died. Others retained the characteristics of birds, reptiles, fish, and mammals. These doctors mixed DNA from various species, hoping for a genetic transformation, but the outcome of their experiment was ugly and horrifying.

Some of the monsters they created were intelligent and superior to humans, so the doctors placed them in separate chambers with their own life support. Then they began work on human cells and DNA. They accelerated the cloning process. Their objective was to create the most perfect being. They arranged the genetic material to produce the perfect human clone.

"This time, no mistakes will occur. We will create the best of best that humanity can produce."

The first human clone was created. After the incubation period, the clone woke. The doctors opened the life support chamber and the clone came out, confused and disoriented. He looked around.

The doctors looked at him and asked, "Are you okay? Can you see us and hear what we are saying? Do you feel anything?"

With an angry sound resembling a growl, he collapsed. The doctors placed him back in the chamber for further examination. The clone was about one and a half meters tall, with a stocky body. His head was large, with dark eyes and serrated teeth similar to a piranha.

At the same time, the female clone woke up. She looked intensely at the doctors, and the doctors looked at her. She was the same as the male clone, but this time they kept the chamber locked.

The doctors were dismayed by what they saw. The error was grave. They needed to begin all over again with different methods. They decided not to tangle with mixing DNA from different species. They experimented with new cells and DNA. The conclusion of every test was the same: no new clones, just new fetuses with no properties for life, just cells. They discarded each of these.

"What can we do now? We created monsters, and we can't return to Earth. What now?"

And so *Eve* continued traveling at speed of sound into the dark, unknown Universe.

Months passed. The doctors and scientists had no clue as to what to do with their creations. Supplies were getting short. They needed to come up with some ideas if they wanted to live and to continue their experiment in cloning. They knew they were lost in space. They built a machine that made oxygen, and another to recycle carbon monoxide. Now they were building a greenhouse. The ship started to looked more and more like a home. They planted produce of all kinds. They genetically engineered animals for the treatment of aliments. Things were looking very promising and exiting. Men and women celebrated with drink and food and love-making, forgetting all about the clones and the monsters they created.

The male clone opened his dark eyes after six and a half months. He looked to his right at the other chamber where he saw the female clone like him. He contacted her telepathically.

Two doctors working in the lab had a funny feeling. They turned and looked at the clones. They started walking towards the chambers. The male clone was using telepathy, controlling the doctors. The doctors opened the chambers.

The two clone moved forth, killing the two doctors. They then took over the craft, using the other humans as slaves.

In time, these clones would have offspring of their own. They will need to find a planet to use as their home, for the craft will not sustain life for a long time.

The clones named themselves. The male called himself "Me," while the female was called "Ma." They learned everything in the craft at a rapid pace. Their minds evolved rapidly. They became carnivores, and one-by-one they ate all the humans in *Eve*. But they preserved the blood of the humans.

The craft was now too small for further life support. They needed to find a planet. After one year of searching, they finally found what looks like a small planet with no life. They landed the craft there. It turned out to be a dead star with a core of solid iron. They resided there for a long time. Using material from the dead star, they began to construct a new craft. Taking documents from the records the humans collected, they created a massive database of knowledge.

With that, the clones and their evolved brains created fantastic machines and a new way of life in the new spacecraft. Food was abundant for all the clones and the beasts they kept. Finally, they departed from the dead star, traveling at the speed of light, searching for a livable planet to sustain them all. Now there were over a million clones that became the Aliens of the entire Universe. But they had no place to call home.

Zero Hour to the End

Chaos, destruction, death. This is the theme on the planet Earth. The disasters continue with no sign of weakening. It seems to be the end of the old planet and the human race. Those alive are in a shock at the unbelievable situation. The humans remaining witness the horror; it is unbearable. There is no place to run for cover or hide from this terrible, dark, hellish end of the human race. Screams and cries of pain and agony fill the air.

This goes on for another 365 day until 0 hour, when it all will be over. A little over 4 billion people remain on Earth. This is one third of the whole human race, waiting for the extermination of the world. No one can change man's destiny. He and only he is responsible for this end, Men became gods, creators of bogus ideas. They dragged their fate into the abysses of hell, and now they want out. They don't want to pay for their mistakes and wrong doing.

The Others (Aliens) return, hovering near the planet Vetuvius, a new discovered planet. They look at Earth and say, "The time has come! Now Orion's belt will take formation, the planets will line up with one another and stop rotating for 66 hour and 6 minutes until 0 hour: the galaxy's adjustment and the planets' revival of new order of the Universe. This change occurs every 250 million years. It is the purification of universal cleansing."

"We have seen everything that we need to know. It is time to go from here. We will not return."

And with that, the Aliens depart at warp speed into infinity.

The Aliens know that if they remain there they would be terminated by the harsh solar winds and the vortex of the spinning of the sun.

There are 60 minutes to 0 hour. On Earth, there is more death and sorrow, pain and agony, deterioration. Everything man-made becomes a thing of the past. They are like zombies, walking with nowhere to go. They have no energy, not even to kill or to eat. The planet is becoming hotter and hotter. The sky is dark. There is no day or night anymore. The only light is the dark red light coming from the sun. Just that and a scorching heat with temperatures in the 50s C and rising.

Something is happening with the Moon. It is turning red and moving faster than before. Humans and beasts all look up. It is a horrifying view. People are crying with sadness and sorrow.

"It is the end of us and our loving planet," they exclaim. They are the last words from the human race.

The planets commence rotating, one by one, in formation. It begins with Mercury, the one closest to the sun, then Venus, and the Earth and Moon. Then Mars, Jupiter, Saturn, Uranus, Neptune, Pluto. The new dwarf planets Haumea, Makemake, Eris, and the newest ones discovered by the Aliens: Vetuvius, Crotonius, and Susej, the farthest from the sun.

The countdown is at 33 minutes to 0 hour.

The Earth now is unprotected by the Moon, and the Earth's magnetic field is in disarray. It offers no protection against the sun's plasma. The sun shoots strong plasmatic flares at the Earth, blasting it with fire that consumes the planet. The remaining humans and all other living creatures are consumed, disintegrated in an instant.

It is 0 hour: the end of the world and the Hu-man race.

The solar system is still. There is no movement and no life, only the roar of the sun and the sound of the Earth's galaxy, thundering across the Universe. This will go on for thousands of years, until it all stops.

The planetary bodies move rapidly in a circular motion, back to their normal positions, which sets up a chain reaction that stabilizes Orion's belt in synchronization with the planets. They align to a new formation and constellation for a new order. Earth is the only planet hit by the sun's bombardment.

On the spacecraft *Adam*, the crew has no knowledge of the destruction of the Earth and the colossal changes that took place millions of kilometers from them. By this time, the clones—now numbering in the thousands—take over the craft. They have more sophisticated control. The human doctors and scientists slowly cease to exist. One by one, men and women are gone. The clones with their kinetic powers transform the old spacecraft into a majestic life support sphere that kept all of them secure and protected from all dangers in the Universe.

The sphere is not a spacecraft with motors and mechanics to propel them from one point to another. The sphere becomes a part of them. In time, the sphere grows to the size of a small planet and can support new clones. These clones are made of a good substance. They are tranquil, peaceful, and strong, with advanced knowledge and telepathic power. They also learn the history of the human race. They study to learn all about the molecules of the Universe and their own bodies' composition. Traveling for eons in time they go from galaxy to galaxy, planet to planet, to find the blue planet, their home.

The search comes to an end.

"This is the galaxy of the blue planet called Earth. It is this one because it has a yellow sun. We will find our home."

They communicate among themselves telepathically. In a blink of an eye, they hover over the planet that was Earth. But something is definitely wrong. Earth is dark with no signs of life. It is a dead planet.

"The last vision was the Earth on fire. But we have lost all knowledge of the matter. But how? We will travel through time to learn what occur to the Earth. We need to know the history of our DNA from the beginning of our creation. But before departing to times past, we are going to create our new planet, our new home."

They send down a sphere packed with nucleic composition of atoms, including animal and plant cells, hydrogen and carbon, and microbes and germs. The sphere is seven kilometers in circumference with the power of 12,000 hydrogen nuclear bombs. When it touches down, a large explosion occurs. From their sphere, they observe and telepathically control the massive explosion caused by the sphere.

The chain reaction spreads around the planet at 700 kilometers per second. In seven seconds, it all ceases. In its place, a large nebula forms.

The strangers bow their heads and with one thought they embrace, saying "Complete."

A short time passes, and the enormous sphere descends to the new Earth, a planet resurrected from the ashes of destruction. It is a new creation, with plants and mountains, rivers and lakes, oceans, birds, fish, and all kinds of mammals walking, flying, and swimming. It is peaceful and beautiful. The new Earth is very green with life.

The Strangers look at all that it is, created from what was not.

"This is our new home, our planet, a part our lives. We will protect it and be the guardians of the Universe. We will stay vigilant. What occurred to the blue planet will not take place here. For all the time to come, this is our planet, our green planet Earth."

New Earth, New Life

The Clone named Primo gets out from the large sphere to test the air for the first time. They are oxygen breathers. He finds air. He just flows through the sphere's wall like it was made of liquid. Primo wears skin-tight overalls made of the same material as the sphere, light metallic silver blue in color. He is covered from head to toe. Covering his eyes is a flat eye protector similar to a visor. Bright colors run across the visor. They change according to the mood of the clone Primo. All the clone males and females have the same material on them. It is a protective second skin. It is controlled by telekinesis, the power of the mind. Every one of them has the powers of telepathy and telekinesis, a power that moves objects and commands all things dead or alive. Their power is unknown.

They are all out of the sphere now, a multitude of thousands upon thousands, male and female, all together in harmony and peace. They start touring the green Earth, with joy like children in a sand box. They are all in the air flying. Everything is green and blue. There are animals of all kinds. Butterflies and birds are everywhere. There are trees, mountains, lakes, and rivers. From above, they look down and see the ocean, a mixture of blues and greens. It looks fantastic. Primo and three other clones survey every centimeter of the land, finding all of it good. Then they dive into the waters. Again, everything is perfect and pure without a single flaw. The three clones will always be together and scout the planets and the Universe for danger.

Primo knows that somewhere out there is malice and destruction, something that will do anything to conquer and control. Primo and his two brothers concur. They call all the others for a meeting to explain the situation at hand and the actions needed to be taken. After the meeting the three of them depart into the past at speed 300,000 times faster than the speed of light. They can go anywhere in the blink of an eye. They will time warp through the Universe to galaxies and strange planets, in and out black holes, through vortices, nuclear gasses, and comets. They hope for the sake of the peaceful new Green Planet and its new life, not to find malice. The concept of time is of no use to them, even though they know and are wary of time and space.

Above the Green Planet, they place thousands of small spheres, like sentinels or guardians, so the planet would be protected from intruders and malicious energy. The order of things is in place. The completion and protection of the planet and the stabilization of life have all been done in a systematic form with mathematical precision.

The strangers together reach a decision to go back in time to find out what caused the Earth's destruction, and to determine why they were made. The clones know almost all of their history, but a small amount of missing knowledge makes them unaware of many facts about themselves and the human race. It is necessary for them to travel back and forth into the past and into future to unveil the truth. The journey is long. The work is vast and complicated. The three of them depart with the life support sphere measuring 100 meters in circumference. And in a blink they return. It is a test of the vessel's speed and preparation for the exploration.

"It was strange. The Earth was the same as it was when we found it a short time ago, scorching hot, covered with lava and no life in this time period. We will remain here in warped time and study the past and future of the old planet Earth. We need to know how it was created, why it was destroyed, and where our DNA originated. There are important facts to document in our records."

Traveling at blink velocity, they go back 250,000,000 years. At this time on planet Earth, there was nothing but vegetation and beasts. They descend, observing and studying the life there.

Then back 550,000,000 years. It is the same manifestation with similar living creatures. They document these, and then go back to 1,555,000,000 BC. Nothing has changed. They observe and study the creatures and plants, but no humans exist. The Strangers look at the whole system. They descend to the Earth and touch the ground. Telepathically, they tunnel into space to find the beginning, the birth of the Earth, billions of years in the past. But it was the same formation. Very little had changed for the Earth geographically.

They collect all the data they find and depart to the future, going to 200,000,000 BC. This is the time of the Jurassic world. Ninety percent of beasts and plants are shaped physiologically different than they are believed to be by later humans. Moving into the future to 100,000,000 BC, it is much the same. Some beasts and plants are somewhat different than in prior times, but again there are no humans or any new kind of life.

"The history recorded by humans is twisted. It is not in accordance with nature."

So they depart from that time, traveling 10,000,000 years into the future.

It is extraordinary to see the changes that the planet Earth had been through. Every time they travel from the past to the future, their knowledge increases and becomes vast and vibrant. In a spectacular time warp, they go into the future by 800,000 years. By now, the formation of the planet has moved into a different shape. The formation of the land now has continents with new forms of animals and plants. The Universe remains the same with no change. It is an intriguing discovery for them about the history of Earth. They continue until they come to the beginning of the human race, when the first man and woman appear. They are roaming the Earth, confused and lost.

"They look human. It is possible that these are the ancestors of all humans. We will go twenty years into the future to monitor their lives and progress."

Primo and his brothers agree. At the same time, they notice a pulsating effect, a rapid motion of intrusion in the Earth's atmosphere. They don't see what is causing it, but they feel something is not right. They look down from above, and they see a man running, scared and confused, towards the desert.

The Strangers leave that period of time and go 150 years into the future, now the Earth is populated with more humans and animals of all kind. With the population of Earth and the increase of living things, it is becoming a different planet. The humans are changing. Their constitution and nature is evolving. The humans have moved from their natural environment. The Strangers see villagers in different parts of the Earth waging wars. There is bloodshed and death.

Again, the Strangers feel the same vibration in space on their travel. They feel uneasy and uncomfortable.

"This is a feeling of malice. Evil doers are around here. We need to find this force immediately before is too late for us and planet Earth."

The feeling of malice in the Universe seems aggressive. It has to be some kind of evil force. But because it is in a different dimension of time, it and the Strangers miss each other. Their time is off by 30 seconds.

Their knowledge of each other and their closeness was as far as a million years apart. They traveled for light years and then return to Earth. They do this often to guard the planet. The Strangers investigate a few years of human time into the future. The wars continue and malice grows, becoming a way of life for the humans. The Strangers, Primo and his two brothers, separate from each other and divide the planet into four corners: Primo goes to the North, Primo C=2 takes the western side, and Primo C=3 goes to the eastern part of Earth. To the south, the sphere sits, controlling all of Planet Earth and the Earth's galaxy. They scout for people with their genetic makeup, but without much success.

"They have some DNA traces similar to ours, but it is not dynamic and strong as we expected. We will go 200 years of man's time into the future and check them out, hoping for some answers. We just need patience and time, human time, to develop and evolve the humans. In time we will find our DNA."

Now it is the year 1200 BC, after the first man the Strangers spotted on the Earth. They search and search. Through the millennia they see that the humans have gone from bad to worse in war, killing, and natural disasters. The DNA they find is weak and far from their own. They continue to scout the future. They observe awful situations for humanity: wars, destruction, and malice all around the planet. They go far into the future once more in a blink. They reach a new time. They see a different planet, completely covered with water.

In a moment, they recognize something is wrong. "We must have passed the time period, or a change has occurred to the planet. The planet is blue!"

They go down into the abyss of the oceans. They saw a horrific view: millions of people and animals dead.

"What happened here? Was it nature's way? Or something more! We transmitted ourselves 6000 years from the first human. We will go back to year 0 and evaluate the evolution of the first humans."

The Strangers go back in time to explore the birth of the planet. They go back trillions of years, accumulating data on the planet. But what they found is that the Earth had existed forever. No time of creation is found. No Big Bang that they had learned from the humans who created them.

"The doctors and scientist were wrong that the Universe was created by a galactic explosion," the Strangers communicate to one another telepathically. "Human history is recorded in reverse. We need to gather data of our own and study the history of the human race, starting in AD 2000 as they recorded and going backwards to the first human. Then the line will be consistent with human DNA."

The Strangers go back every five years. They find the history from AD 2000 to 1 BC, recorded by humans. They have no clue why the calculation is backwards. They travel back from year 1 BC to year 4000 BC. Again they see a small village with humans, but this time it is different. They go around the planet, observing that the waters are lower, mountains more visible, and all kind of animals are rooming the Earth. It is beautiful and peaceful, nothing like the past and the future that they know.

The Search Continues

The Strangers then transport into the future to the year 3900. They see people working to build pyramids. It is stressful, but even there they found very little trace of the DNA that they are looking for.

The population is Egyptian. The Strangers remain there for a short while to oversee the accomplishments of this new race. They remain there for 100 years of human time, which is 10 minutes their time.

Again, they miss the Others by 30 seconds. They pass each other with the same energy as before in the other dimension of warped time. Both adversaries feel something,

Primo exclaims to his brothers with concern, "That malice again! And it is stronger. We need to take rapid measures."

They depart quickly into space to search, remaining in space for 1000 years of human time, one hour of their time. They then return to Earth and telepathically view the planet's core and its atmosphere for any signs of malice surrounding the Earth's solar system. The outcome is inconclusive, but they stay alert and vigilant.

The year now is 3500 BC according to human records.

They descend and see the place is a vast area of greens, with trees, mountains, rivers, and animals everywhere.

"This place is different from the other one. The people here are different, but somewhat the same. The way of life here is in solitude and hard work. They also have an incredible intelligence. Something is wrong!"

They are confused by what they see. It is not a pleasant view. On the top of a pyramid, the natives are sacrificing a human by draining its blood. The Strangers look at the action. Puzzled, they go away with no intervention. They can change history here but they know it will be in vain, so they go back in time to the year 3800 at the first home of the Egyptians in Egypt. The Strangers are hit with a stunning scene. Only a few people are alive, and all the buildings are covered with sand. There is destruction for that race. That history was not recorded. It was not in the records of human history. They hover over the land for a short time, and then descend to the ground. They approach the people and communicate telepathically with them.

The Strangers ask, "What occurred here?"

The people exclaim with fear and horror, "The Others did this! Incredible destruction and the death of thousands of our people just because we were short of our quota for material supplies."

"Who are they?" they ask.

"The Others? Like you, but different!"

Primo connects with his two brothers. They become one for the power of absorbing the information of the natives into a visual form. They see a storm of sand. First it looks more like a tornado, and then a wave about 500 meters high, burying the land about to a depth of 100 meters, leaving the tips of only three pyramids. The Primos can't make a preliminary assessment on the matter, but they know it was not caused naturally. A force from outside nature inflicted the destruction. They detect a force of malice in that region.

Primo feels the identity of this malice, just as he did before.

They can't ignore the situation at hand. They depart on to the future, to 3300. By now they recognize that everywhere on Earth buildings are constructed in a square with mathematical precision. They investigate it and discover peculiar geometric lines and tunnels inside the pyramids in Egypt and those of the Maya. In Africa and China, all over the planet they find signs of different shape and design.

"It is what we feared! Something out there has been controlling the humans for thousand of human years! But why?"

In a blink, they are in the future, in the 2200 BC. Earth is a changed place. The human population is larger and more spread over the entire planet. Now they have continents, countries, and colonies for many races. They begin to be divided among themselves.

The Strangers continue the search for their DNA line among all humans of the Earth. What they find is minuscule. They go ahead with their plan into the future. Their calculations lead them to 1100 BC. In Italy, there is a race of people, strong warriors and hard workers.

The country has an abundance of natural resources. The people are intelligent, progressing in construction and discovery.

In their travels, the Strangers come across a similar race called the Greeks. Their genetic makeup is almost the same as the Italians. The Strangers know all about their history, how they brought a world of civilization, order, and progress in all aspect of life.

Again they leap to the future, to 950 BC. A new government is being formed in Italy, a new empire called Romanus. They have order and a system, as well as the most dominating army on the planet. The leader is a man with a superior intellect. He has accomplished many things for Italy and the Romanus Empire. His name is Claudius Augustus Caesar.

"His intelligence is superior to the other men."

Stupefied, the Strangers look at one another. "The Others are clever. They have a special power and ways of manipulating people and history. We will take Claudius for our DNA sample."

That night, Claudius is out on the palace balcony. The Moon is dim; the night is dark. He looks up and sees a bright round sphere descending from the sky, suspended in the air. It gets close to him. He remains paralyzed on the spot. The Strangers, Primo and his brothers, exit from the sphere, floating toward Claudius.

They say in Latin, "Don't be afraid! We are friends!"

Claudius responds with fear and amazement. "You speak my language!"

"Yes," they respond. "We speak all languages"

"What do you want from me?"

"A simple tag of hair, if it is okay with you."

The Strangers extract one simple hair from Claudius's head and depart into the future. They arrive in 700 BC in the same territory in the city of Rome. There they encounter a centurion by the name of Gaius Petrus Marius, a valiant Roman centurion. This man is the ancestor of Captain Gaius Marius of the second-century Roman military, who developed the greatest Roman military power. The Strangers extract hair from him as well, and analyze it. The results are conclusive. This genetic line matches their own DNA.

Pleased with the results, they depart into the future year, arriving in Rome in 1996. From there they roamed the Earth to get in contact with the future humans and find the direct descendents with the same DNA, someone from Gaius's blood line in this new generation. The right genetic information will signal the end of their search.

They travel in the blink of an eye to the four corners of Planet Earth, but nowhere do they find a connection. They continue for 100 years of human time, equal to 10 minutes of the Strangers' time. Then Primo and his brothers brainstorm, searching telepathically. The answer materializes in front of them. They see a man sitting under a fig tree, relaxing. The place is a farm in the southern region of Italy called Calabria. They have a strong feeling, and they know that this is their man. They begin to study his life from that moment on, into the future and back. They want to make sure this time that he is the one they are looking for. His blood line must be 100% compatible with theirs.

The three of them inside the sphere hover around for moment. The sphere becomes bright and soft to the eye. They descend, and the three of them float toward the man sitting against the tree. They take him and depart from Earth. The Strangers d0 that at the same time for the rest to the planet Earth, searching for the perfect DNA, but this is the one man they are seeking.

In a quantum of time at high velocity, traveling into the infinity of the Universe, they pass a spacecraft the size of a small planet. They feel the malice inside it. That craft is traveling at the speed of light toward the planet Earth. Telepathically, the three of them probe the craft. They see the malice, their enemy. Now they know what to do to protect the Green Planet. They hope for a time that the Earth will be safe.

"The malice is strong! Coming from within! We need to endure a hard labor to take care of this matter. We must penetrate into the bottom of this creation and eradicate the malice from them!"

In the meantime, the Others reach Earth. They hover 234,000 kilometers above the Moon, observing the humans and their self-destruction. The year is 1996. They remain there for a few seconds of the Alien's time, which is a week of human time.

"It is all in accordance with our expectation and plan, rearranging Earth and its nature to our liking. We shall come back in the future. For now, we go forth in search of that invisible brilliant gas ball."

They speed into the dark Universe, leaving behind the planet Earth.

Warning Signs

The Strangers return to Earth with the man they called Gianni. He is still comatose. They set him next to the fig tree.

(This is the beginning of the story told by Gianni in the first book in this series, *Clones: Aliens or Us?*)

They flash back to the past to the year 1964. The world is in chaos with wars zone. Combat is taking place on the continent of Asia. They look in distress and sadness at the human race and the havoc it constantly making for itself.

Primo and his brothers have a plan.

"We need to help them if we want to save the Earth. The malicious force here is powerful and beyond their knowledge. They will eradicate themselves. Their end is evident. We will do all we can through Gianni. There is a chance. We can't change their history, but with signs from us they can perhaps stop the madness that is coming to their future."

From that time until the year 2012, humans discovered all sorts of signs and symbols from within the planet.

In mountains, beneath the oceans, and in the stars, they find new knowledge, leading to inventions. Creativity and engineering increased. Blind as they were, their abilities were not sufficient to recognize the information left by the Strangers. Code after code was too hard for humans to comprehend or use for the good of the human race.

The most advance signs were the crop circles and the underwater creations that the Strangers left behind. An important message to the humans was the crystal skull. In it was one of the most critical pieces of information to be discovered by humans, but it took time for this new knowledge to be recognized. In the mind of humans, the skull was false, a fake. They did not study the skull with good intentions. Later, other crystal skulls were discovered. Archeologists concluded that all the skulls were forgeries, and so they left them on shelves.

The other sign that the Strangers left for humans to use to find out about the danger and conflict for the planet Earth and the human race was through dolphins. They were the most intelligent of all living creatures, with a language in a code by them:

... ‾. .. ‾ ‾ ‾. ‾ ... . ‾ .‾.‾‾..‾‾..‾.‾... .‾

Humans knew about the clicking sound of the dolphins, but they did not recognize it as a code. They did not discover the Strangers' message.

Another sign given by the Strangers was a new crop circle that appeared around AD 2000. Again, humans thought nothing about the new circle for years. It was the Europeans who discovered how to use them. This circle with new knowledge made possible what became known as Utopiaromana. It was mathematically represented as C.L.O.N.E.S+=2MC2+A=D.EX.T.0=B-MMIL=T.

The Strangers also left a particular code for the people of Earth so they could be ready for the end of their existence and the destruction of the blue planet.

Gianni did what he could to convince the leaders of the world, with very little. And then communication from Gianni and his new family, the Strangers, was severed by Gianni's death. And so the end of the human race came. They were gone forever.

Life will continue on this planet with a new beginning, but it will take millions years. It will come about because of the new race of Strangers, who were the dream and creation of humanity. A new race of perfect beings will emerge with a better intellect, people superior to the old humanity, the clones of humanity.

The Strangers now arrive at the Green Planet, their home, where they reunite with all of the others. They share their knowledge about the events they had seen in the Universe and life in the past of the planet Earth, including the beginning of their blood line and the source of their DNA.

Primo begins the conversation by explaining the history of the planet Earth and the coming of humanity. "The time was beyond measure, an infinite amount of time that we will never know. That was when the creation of the Earth and the Earth's galaxy took place."

Primo continues describing their exploration of the planet Earth and its galaxy. Now they have to make plans to protect their Green Planet from the malicious force they know. It is a force with which they will have contact sometime soon.

Primo explains this to his entire family of 144,000,000 clones.

"The time has come. We know the consequences. We need to act quickly. We can't wait much longer!"

At the same time, they all agree. Soon, they take their positions. They all know what to do. They feel the malicious energy coming like a storm of destruction.

Primo and Prima together look at their home, the Green Planet.

The Watch-Clone

Primo expresses his care with regard to the lives of his large family of clones.

"If we don't stay vigilant and be the guardians of the Universe, we will have the same fate as our ancestors, not by our own hand but by the malicious ones. I feel that they will find our planet in a short time."

Prima, with a refined demeanor and calm attitude says, "I will help in all tasks for the protection of our planet and all lives we have here, to save us all from this malicious force."

Primo agrees with her and replies, "You will keep the order of things here. The three of us will take our place in space, and together we will secure our home."

In an instant, the Green Planet becomes a metallic, silver-blue sphere, like a protective shield. Inside, everything is normal. Anything can get out, but nothing except the clones can get in. Primo and his two brothers fly to the three points of the Universe to explore the vast area of space, looking for the malicious and destructive energy. They roam their galaxy for a thousand years, but find not one single sign of malice. After they return, they come together and reach the decision that Primo will depart for Earth to collect the history of humanity and all living things on planet Earth.

In the meantime, in a galaxy far away from the Green Planet, the Others hover over planet after planet, hoping to discover new colonies of people from whom they can take resources. They arrive at a new galaxy with two red stars and millions of planets and moons. They remain there to explore. They need minerals for their survival. They will do whatever is necessary.

The mother craft sends out hundreds of small craft to scout the new planets. Each travels at the speed of light, circling the planets one by one. The only materials discovered are gases, sulfur, solar radiation, dynamic pressure from solar winds, and electromagnetic fields. The craft returns to the mother craft with empty hands. The search ends there.

In a quantum leap, they move on to a different solar system smaller than the one before. There is no star to be seen. It looks like dead stars with dead planets. They inspect over 10,000 planets, finally encountering a large planet and a galaxy that resembles the Earth's solar system. The gigantic planet has gases and an extremely high temperature. Circling the planet are rings along with thousands of moons.

The Others get as close as possible with the large mother craft. They send a probe to extract matter from the large planet. The only matter from the extraction is melted iron and rocks, nothing but lava.

"The composition of this planet will be useful in the construction of new craft and the refit of the mother craft into a larger ship with more comfortable spaces to enhance our quality of life."

They call the new planet Lavaferreus.

So they remain there for some time and retrieve millions upon millions of tons of material. Afterwards, the main clone, Me, exclaims with an angry tone and a savage roar like a beast, "We will find another Earth-like planet, with natives and minerals that we need for our survival. It is our obligation and responsibility."

Before they depart from that dead zone, Me decides to play with the power of the mother craft. He sends down a shock wave, more powerful than 2,500,000 nuclear bombs, to eradicate one of the dead planets. It pleases him greatly to play god. He is full of malice.

When the planet is hit, the impact crushes the crust. A massive explosion occurs in the core of the planet, shooting billions of chunks of the planet into space on the other side of the alien craft, destroying the planet.

They depart from there, passing through a black hole into a different dimension. They arrive at the Earth's galaxy, and the Earth's solar system. This time, the formation of the planet is somewhat different. They are a bit confused and dismayed in that regard.

"Where are we?" Me questions the partners in charge of the craft, those responsible for navigation and mapping.

"We are back at the Earth's galaxy, 2,000,000 years into the future of what was planet Earth."

"Excellent!" Me replies. "We will track the Earth and all other planets for life. This time we will stay here. This galaxy is rich in minerals and possible new life.

They will travel from the first star to the end star of the Earth's galaxy to find and consume all the resources of the planets, then destroy them just for entertainment. But it will take time, a long time. They will find many obstacles in their path, but the malice they bring with them will be fearful and wreak havoc everywhere they go.

What will they do if they find the Strangers from the Green Planet? Will they do the same thing they did to the humans and planet Earth?

Do they know of the Strangers existence? Do they know of their powers?

What will happen?

Will the Strangers know about the Others in time?

What kind of battle will take place in the Universe? What will be the fate of the planets? The Others have the power to destroy anything, including planets.

This will be the Universal Cosmic Galactic War for the survival of creation.

Who will win?

It is good versus evil. Victory will determine the fate of the Universe.

You will find out the answers to these questions in the next book in the ongoing story of *Clones*.

It will be a spectacular confrontation, a conflict between the two supreme powers. Will the Universe have a protective guardian or an evil destroyer? Who will be the winner of this conflict? Will one of them be destroyed? Is the Universe at an end or not?

To be continued

Next: *Clones: Strangers Versus the Others—Conflict*

Epilogue

For the planet Earth and the human race, everything came to an end, but only because of the stupidity, ignorance, greed, and a desire to be god. All of this killed man. Since creation, humans have always tried to change their surroundings, to make them better than what God provided. Through the centuries, history tells us how humanity is evolving from bad to worse. They will go to the extremes of life for a change. They conquer and hold dominion through power and lies.

Man will deceive himself, making things up, fantasizing about how to become God. To be eternal, he invents and creates, builds and destroys.

When Adam disobeyed God, he endured all the consequences for all creation. The human race now pays for his disobedience, and they will until the end of humanity. All humans know that there is no turning back. They will go ahead with their plans no matter the outcome, even to self-annihilation.

Humans commence with the most devastating act of the human race, disobedience. They then move on to killing and stealing, ravishing and raping his own kind. From that, they continue to innovations, inventions, compositions, and integration of matter, mixing and matching chemicals. Exploiting the Earth for minerals and precious material, they will not stop. Their mind is set. They will inflict diseases on themselves and all living creatures.

Every decade brings new innovations and creations: from weapons at close range to terrible long-range weapons of mass destruction; from the discovery of fire to the destructive fire; from hunting for food to hunting for extermination of his kind and creation; from the survival of life to the conquest of power and the end of life.

Humans will become kings of kingdoms, emperors over empires, and presidents of countries. They work with determination for power and the control of the race. Everyone—the simple man, the underdog, the worker and the slave—are dominated by governments and mighty man-made gods.

Humans strive for higher heights that they can leap. With the invention of machines—from the steam engines and propellers, to combustion and nuclear fusion—they create the power of the sun.

Advances in the age of microchips give humans the ability to go where they have never been before. They will not know where they will go next. Their knowledge will surpass their direction of accomplishments, and the electronic age will conquer them and control his mind. Humans will not be satisfied with what they have done. They want more; they want faster. They reach the point of transforming themselves to perfection. Humans have been researching cloning for decades. It began in the early 1900s, first with plants, then with animals, and finally with people. Genetic engineering of the human cell is the change that will lead humans to the end of their existence on planet Earth.

This is not science fiction. It is reality. Really. I tell you it will occur sooner rather than later.

Humans are losing their minds, first with morals, family separation, abortion, cheating, lies, and the loss of the most important ingredient in their life: God.

Warning . . . Warning . . . Warning

This book is not for sensitive people or children.

Even though this story is fiction, a creation from someone's imagination, this book can be disturbing and horrifying. The content describe the horror and the terror of the Earth and all living creatures being consumed. In all its aspects, this is just impossible to comprehend.

The possibility remains that this could occur.

The future for humanity is bleak and deadly. Self-annihilation is the destination of the human race.

Judgment is a fact. Punishment is upon us. Deliverance is at hand, not by our own doing, but through God's actions. The warnings are vivid. Time is short. It could be now, today or tonight. Humans are taking their time in this world for granted, but for the past 100 years humans have created a more complicated world, moving mountains, digging thousands of miles of tunnels, sucking natural resources such as oil, gold, silver, and precious minerals. They cut trees, destroying forests. They convert materials just for the pleasure of manufacturing homes, bridges, skyscrapers, and all kinds of machines. They also use them to make instruments of destruction. They glamorize themselves with riches and elegant furniture, so they can be comfortable as kings.

Humanity has little regard for the creation of God. They take and take from Earth, but give very little back.

They suck the Earth's minerals, moving mountains and making tunnels. They also kill one another. They kill animals. They are destroying the oceans and exterminating the whales and other precious ocean life just for their raw materials, which they use for decoration. They have anointed themselves as gods.

They will go on and on. There is no stopping; the course is set. For the majority of the human race, it is too late.

Humanity is doomed. False prophets will emerge with lies, deceiving people. They are self-proclaimed messengers of God.

No one can predict the end or judgment day. Only God knows.

Men need to take care of planet Earth and stop messing around with things. He should not stick his nose into things that are not his.

Humans need to stop deceiving themselves and playing god. They are fooling themselves.

Acknowledgements

The All Mighty God. God is truth the truth can't be changed.

Thanks to my Master and Teacher, Jesus Christ, for the knowledge given to me and for my life in this world. All my good accomplishments are because of Him, my God.

I want to thank my beautiful mother and father for my existence and the love they always had for their family. Rest in peace, Mamma.

My special appreciation and thanks goes to my beautiful wife, Cheryl, my daughter, Nina, and my son, John for their support, love, and patience.

To my sisters and brother: I love you.

I would like to thank you for buying this book. I hope you will enjoy it. Please look for other intriguing action and science fiction novels coming soon from MR Comics & Art.

Upcoming Publications

For information on upcoming publication
of new books, comics, statues, and
other collectibles, visit our web site at
w.w.w.mrcomicsandart.com.

Clones: Aliens or Us?

The first book in the Clones trilogy

Available from MR Comics & Art and Amazon.com

Comics and Graphic Novels

CPSIA information can be obtained at www.ICGtesting.com
Printed in the USA
BVOW040933030712

294220BV00001B/1/P